Author's Note

I first walked into Anfield in the Autumn of 1970.
I was ten years old.

I suppose it would be fair to say that it was love at first sight and the love affair is still going strong 30 years down the road. Some people say that football is something that you grow out of, a bit like tomato ketchup I suppose. Well it never worked that way with me. As a season ticket holder for the last 25 years I have seen the highs and the lows. I was on the Kop for the St Etienne game in '77 when the noise nearly blew the roof off. And then I was on the Leppings Lane terrace at Hillsborough in 89 when the sky fell in, but at end of a storm there's a golden sky . . . well, let's hope so.

I'm glad to report that both my boys, Dyonne and Courtney, seem to be well and truly bitten by the bug. To be honest they have had a pretty torrid time over recent years. Both have had to endure endless hours of crowing and gloating from the United fans in their class but I'm glad to report they have held firm and they are both staunch Liverpool fans. My dad took me, I take them, and so it goes on down the generations. Maybe when I am dead and buried and long gone some future relative will be able to read this and still share the love of the game.

I hope that my love of football as a whole and Liverpool in particular comes through in the pages that follow. It's supposed to be a childen's book but it seems to appeal to all ages. Enjoy it.

Mark Frankland
April 2000

D1428144

The
drums
of Anfield

Mark Frankland

*To Louise,
with all best wishes,*

August 2000

Glenmill

A Glenmill Publication

©Mark Frankland, 2000
The moral right of the author has been asserted

All rights reserved. No part of this publication may be
reproduced or transmitted in any form or by any means,
electronic or mechanical, including photocopying, recording
or any information storage or retrieval system, without
prior permission in writing from the publishers.

First published in 2000

Glenmill
Dumfries
Scotland
DG2 8PX

tel: 01387 730 655
http://www.glenmill.freeserve.co.uk

British Library Cataloguing in Publication Data.
A catalogue record of this book is available from the British Library.

ISBN 0 9535944 2 4

Design, Layout & Typesetting by Ψasmin
email: books@yazzy.net

Cover Photo: John Cocks

*"Some people say that football
is a matter of life and death . . .
. . . but it's much more important than that."*

Bill Shankly

Acknowledgements

To Carol who is always there
to tell me I can do this

To my boys who were
my first audience

To Mum and Dad and Peter
for backing it

To Yasmin for putting up
with ridiculous deadlines

And to Tommy Smith, Ian Callaghan,
Ray Kennedy, Kevin Keegan,
Joey Jones, Terry Mac, King Kenny,
Graham Souness, Phil Thompson,
Alan Hansen, Barney Rubble,
Ian Rush, Steve McMahon, John Barnes,
Ronnie Whelan, John Aldridge,
Jamie Carragher, Sami Hyppia . . .

. . . all those players who
every time they pull on a red shirt
make each and every one of us glad
that we follow the greatest team on earth

———— Contents ————

CONTENTS

CHAPTER ONE

Old Trafford in September

The ball was clipped through from the right back. Tony reacted instantly. He flew across the pitch and slid toward the ball . . . it was gone. Brad Finnighan took it right off Tony's boot and sprinted towards the goal.

A deafening 'Ooooooh!' poured down from the packed stands as Finnighan blasted his shot inches over the bar.

The near-miss switched the noise of the crowd up to a new ear-splitting level. Tony heaved himself off the ground and stood bent over with his hands on his knees. He tried to drag air into his lungs and his heart was pounding painfully. He glanced up at the scoreboard and saw to his relief that there were only seconds to go before half-time.

His left leg was burning with pain. He mentally cursed his manager for insisting that he played even though his leg wasn't properly healed.

He felt a hand ruffle his hair and turned around sharply. It was Finnighan. Brad Finnighan, the 21 year old Irishman who was Manchester United's new pin-up boy.

"Bit tired are we Hobbo. Well it's a hard game for an old man."

Tony snarled but before he had a chance to say anything Finnighan was gone. He caught the signal from the keeper and drifted into the centre circle. The ball was rolled to Helmut Klein, Liverpool's new German centre-half. As he held the ball Tony made a fast break to the edge of the centre circle. Klein clipped the ball forward towards him. It was perfect. Tony saw from the corner of his eye that Bobby Simms, his centre-forward, was making his break exactly on cue.

It was a move that they had practised hard in training. All Tony needed to do now was to flick a curled ball down the left wing and Simms was clear. He moved easily to the ball but his leg let him down. As he was about to make the pass a red-hot pain lanced up his leg and he miss-hit his pass horribly.

Instead of curling down the wing the ball flew into the crowd. A wave of mockery and laughter poured down from the stands.

The referee blew his whistle. Half-time. At last.

As Tony made his way off the pitch he concentrated hard on not limping. The crowd were taunting him and he tried to blot the noise out.

As Finnighan trotted past him he shouted "Nice ball old man." and laughed. Tony gritted his teeth and doggedly made his way toward the tunnel.

Once inside the dressing room he flopped down onto the bench and hung a towel over his head. He allowed the wave of tiredness to wash over him.

Tony Hobbes was 33 and he had played for Liverpool since the age of 19. For the last three seasons he had been the club captain. He was a central midfielder. He had never been known as a flair player, he was a hard-tackling ball winner. He had been issued his fair share of yellow cards in his time. In his mid-twenties he had been a regular in the England side for three years and had collected 27 international caps.

His hundred per cent effort and his crunching tackling had always made him a great favourite of the Liverpool crowd. Whenever he clattered an opponent the supporters would always gleefully chant "Hobbo! Hobbo!"

However this season he was finding that every game was getting harder. His pace had deserted him and he was having to rely more and more on his experience and instinct. To compensate for his loss of speed he had started to play in a deeper and more defensive role. A strong tackle in an away trip to Hillsborough had left him with a badly bruised Achilles heel. He had missed four games and felt that he needed at least another three games off before the injury was properly healed.

Bill Jones, the manager, had collared him on Thursday and had insisted that he should play at Old Trafford. Tony had argued long and hard but Jones would not budge. The United game was vital, he had to play and that was that. He had also reminded Tony that his contract was due for re-negotiation at the end of the season and that he did not look fondly upon players who shirked their responsibilities, especially the captain.

Jones had been brought in as the new manager at the beginning of the season and already most of the players were sick to death of him. He was a Londoner and he believed in absolute discipline. He refused ever to listen to the views of the senior players. He had forced the team to play a more physical game which was beginning to upset the supporters.

Tony had been tempted to tell him exactly what he thought of him but he had managed to hold his tongue. At 33 he had no wish to move clubs. After 14 years Liverpool was in his blood and his son was happily settled in school. He had held his temper and had agreed to play through the pain.

He had been given the job of closing down Brad Finnighan and he had chased the young prodigy around the Old Trafford pitch until he felt that his lungs would burst.

As he sat under his towel he had to admit to himself that the young Irishman had so far had the best of the battle. However all was not lost. By a mixture of luck and desperate defending Liverpool had managed to keep a clean sheet and as long as the score was 0–0 there was always hope.

Jones was hopping mad and yelling at the players. Tony closed his eyes and did his best to block out the sound. The manager ripped the towel from his head and threw it across the room.

" . . . And you Hobbo, what do you think you're doing? Finnighan's making a mug of you. You're supposed to be the captain. I want effort. I want commitment. Now stop poncing about and get stuck in!"

Tony felt like hitting him. He really did. He could feel the temper rising up in his chest. He took a long deep breath, then got slowly to his feet and went to pick up his towel. The manager watched him in silence for a moment and then launched into an attack on the right full back. Tony called over Ken Timpson, the trainer."

"How is it Hobbo?"

"Lousy. I need another jab."

Timpson frowned. "Are you sure that's a good idea?"

Tony sighed. Of course it wasn't a good idea. It was an awful idea. He had met lots of retired players who were nearly crippled because they had played through their injuries by having too many pain killing injections.

"No it isn't a good idea but there isn't any choice. If I'm supposed to chase that little Irishman around the park for another 45 minutes I'm going to need something."

He winced as the needle was pushed into his leg and then allowed the numbness to spread. It was better. It was by no means good, but at least it was better. A bell rang outside in the corridor. He couldn't believe it. The fifteen minutes of half-time seemed to have gone by in a flash. Reluctantly he heaved himself to his feet and clapped his hands.

"OK boys, heads up. We stopped them in the first half. We can stop them again. Just keep concentrating and ignore the crowd. Let's do it."

As he ran out onto the pitch he felt a little better. The effects of the injection were doing him a power of good. Again he clapped his hands and urged the players on.

For twenty minutes things went well. Liverpool at last managed to get hold of the ball and they began to enjoy some decent periods of possession. United started to show signs of frustration. They started to hoof long balls forward which the Liverpool defence dealt with easily. Suddenly things were looking a lot more hopeful.

Liverpool were steadily building up an attack down the left when Brad Finninghan intercepted a pass and darted forward. Tony threw himself into the challenge, but realised that he was too late a split second before he crashed into Finnighan's legs. The stadium erupted into a barrage of angry sound. Tony got up and waited nervously for the referee. The seconds ticked by with agonising slowness as the crowd bayed "OFF! OFF! OFF!" The ref reached into his pocket and pulled out a card. A wave of relief poured over Tony when he saw that the card was yellow. The crowd booed out their anger.

"Careful Hobbo," said the referee. "One more like that and you're off."

The booking took away Liverpool's rhythm and United started to pile on the pressure again. In the seventy-second minute a slick move resulted in Finnighan sprinting towards the goal. Tony moved in but realised at the last moment that once again he was too late. He just managed to pull out of the challenge that would have seen him sent off. The young Irishman swept past him and buried the ball into the far corner of the net.

The stadium erupted. Tony looked around his players and saw that their heads were down. He tried to encourage them but they already looked a beaten side. For a further ten minutes United piled on wave after wave of attacks and it was getting harder and harder to keep them out. Again Finnighan burst through but this time he kicked the ball slightly too far ahead of himself. Tony lunged at the ball. To his horror and amazement the Irishman seemed to gain a miraculous turn of speed to clip the ball away from him.

Everything then went into a horrible slow motion. Tony was fully committed to the tackle and could do nothing to stop it. He scythed through Finnighan's legs and the Irishman went down as if he had been hit by a tank.

"OFF! OFF! OFF! . . . "

As Tony tried to get up he felt a terrible pain shoot up through his leg. The tackle had done something dreadful to his injury. He had never known an injury to hurt as much.

The ref was making his way across and reaching into his pocket. This time there was no doubt about what colour the card would be. The crowd was jubilant. The pain and the tension and tiredness made Tony feel almost dizzy.

And then Finnighan was there. Up close. Pushing his face close to Tony's. "Is that all you're good for old man? Is that all you can do you old codger? You're nothing but a carthorse, a useless nigger cart horse . . . "

Something snapped. The pain, the manager, the crowd, the mocking Irish voice, the referee pulling out a red card, the racist jibe . . . all of a sudden it was too much. Tony was not aware of making any decision. He just did it. He hit Finnighan hard on the nose and felt the bone crack.

He never looked back. He completely ignored the pain in his leg and jogged in a straight line to the tunnel.

CHAPTER TWO

Bad Sunday

Somebody was shaking his shoulder. Tony came awake in a towering bad mood. Was there no peace to be had anywhere? His mood eased as he opened his eyes to see the face of his son, Ben.

"Oh Ben, do you have to? Just leave me for a little bit can you, what's the time anyway?"

"Ten past eight."

"Well give me until nine will you?"

Ben assumed an unhappy expression. "I can't"

"Why?"

"Cos Grandad's here. I came to warn you."

Tony groaned and sank back into the pillows. He winked at his son and said. "Try and fend him off for a bit will you Ben."

"'Course I will Dad, but . . ."

They both heard the heavy footsteps as Tony's father thundered his way up the stairs. The bedroom door flew open and Winston Hobbes stormed into the room.

"Benjamin, you go out now. You go out and wait downstairs with them women. Me and your daddy need to do some talkin'."

Ben gave his dad a sheepish glance then made his way out of the room and quietly closed the door behind him. Tony sat up painfully and eyed his father. There was little doubt that Winston Hobbes cast an impressive figure. He was six feet six tall and built like a battleship. As was the case every Sunday, he was wearing his best three-piece suit, a starched white shirt and a severe tie. As ever, it did not matter to Winston that his son was a mere six feet away – he shouted as if he were somewhere in Birkenhead on the other side of the Mersey.

"What is goin' on here boy? Why are you skulkin' and sulkin' in your bed. Get up man. No good hidin' yourself away. Get up and face things like a man. I'm not havin' no son of mine hidin' away in his bed like some two bit cringin' coward just because . . . "

Tony held up his hands to try and stem the tide.

"Easy dad, it's only eight o'clock and it *is* Sunday."

"Course I know that boy. I know that because I should be goin' to church to pray to the Lord, not havin' to come round here to sort out business."

Tony's face became suspicious. "What business Dad?"

"Your business boy. What else? Now you might think that you can hide away and pretend that nothin' has gone on, but not me. I am your father and I am your agent too. I have talked to Mr. Jones and I have talked to the

Chairman too. We are seeing them both down at the club at 10.30 and we are goin' to sort things out."

"Oh Dad, did you have to . . . "

"Course I had to boy, now get up out of that bed and get yourself ready. And take care to dress up smart because there are reporters waitin' in the road. Now move it."

Winston turned military-style and walked out. Tony wondered how it was that he was still being bossed about by his dad at the age of 33. How many other men had to put up with a dad like his? Not many. There again, how many men had a dad like his? Not many.

Tony had never met anyone quite like his father. He had got off the boat from Barbados in 1958 and had never left Liverpool. He had found work on the docks and had been there ever since. The other Scouse dockers had soon learned that it was a bad idea to take the Mickey out of the giant West Indian. Over the years many had found out the hard way that it was a very bad idea to get on the wrong side of Winston Hobbes.

It was not just his colour that set him apart from most of his workmates. He also didn't drink or smoke and never missed church on a Sunday. However he gradually became a figure of great respect. As the years passed he became one of the most senior figures in the dockers' union.

When Tony had signed for Liverpool on YTS terms, his father had informed the club that he would act as his agent. Initially Tony had grave misgivings about the arrangement but he hadn't dared mention them to his father. These worries soon passed. Years of bargaining on behalf of the Union had made Winston Hobbes a very hard man to do business with. His powerful presence ensured that Tony always seemed to get a better contract than many of his fellow players. There were very few men

11

around who would get the better of his father.

As he heaved himself out of bed and hobbled to the shower, he grudgingly admitted to himself that his father was right. It was far better to go and face the music rather than hiding away and waiting for the trouble to come to him.

As he allowed the hot water to wake him up he shuddered at the thought of how much trouble there was going to be. As he had sat in the dressing room the afternoon before he had heard the Old Trafford crowd roar a further three times in the last ten minutes. Without Tony to shore them up, the defence had caved in and United had gone on to win 4–0. It was a humiliation. The worst defeat of a Liverpool team at Old Trafford in living memory.

Things had gone from bad to worse. A quick examination of his leg had shown that he had ripped a ligament and would be out of action for at least four months. The other players had barely said a word to him as they trudged into the dressing room. Jones had been almost beside himself with rage. Tony knew that he had really wanted to yell at him but instead he simply said, "I'll sort you out later Hobbes. By God I will." To make things worse, he had been pelted with fruit and coins as he had hobbled out of the ground and onto the team coach.

Later that night he had sat with his wife Karen and watched *Match of the Day*. It had been a miserable experience. Each of his late tackles on Finnighan was shown over and over again in slow motion. They showed his punch six times. The United manager had been livid and demanded a severe punishment. Jones had promised the cameras that Liverpool would be conducting a full enquiry and that disciplinary measures would be taken. Brad Finnighan had given an interview from behind a plaster cast on his broken nose. Both of his eyes had blackened and he had looked an awful mess. The panel in the studio all agreed that what Tony Hobbes had done was a disgrace to the game and that he should be severely punished. The FA had promised an enquiry.

Karen hadn't bothered to leave the television on for the last game. She clicked it off with the remote control and folded her arms.

"Well Tony, I don't think that you are the most popular footballer in England today."

"No."

"And I don't suppose they will be wanting you to do any *Coca Cola* adverts for a little while."

"No."

"But at least the worst is over."

Tony groaned. "No it isn't. The worst is still to come."

Karen smiled sadly. "Oh yes. Sorry. I forgot. Your Dad."

"Yes. My Dad. He's going to kill me."

As Tony hopped into the kitchen the silence was deafening. Winston was sitting bolt upright on a stool gazing fiercely into space. Ben was sitting at the table picking at his cereal. Karen and his mum were making coffee.

At the sight of her hopping son, his mother said in her native Liverpool accent. "Are you all right our Tony? What have you done?"

He smiled at his mother. "Ligaments mum. I've torn them. I won't be playing for a while."

"More than he deserves," Growled Winston. "He deserves to have his leg cut off."

Ben's eyes widened in alarm. Winston noticed and ruffled his hair. "I'm only jokin' boy. Only jokin'. Now you get on and eat that breakfast all up now. When you've finished go and find that walkin' stick that your Daddy used when he broke his ankle. He can't go hoppin' around like some jumpy cat in front of all those newspaper reporters, now can he?"

The big man could not help but smile as he looked down into Ben's worried face. "Don't you worry boy, me and your Daddy are goin' to sort everythin' out."

Tony climbed onto the stool next to his father with difficulty and took a sip of coffee. He glanced at the back page of the paper then pushed it away. Predictably it was dominated by a huge photo of him landing his punch on Finnighan's nose.

Winston glanced down at the photo. "Tell me Tony. Why did you do this thing? You've never done a thing like this before."

"I don't know Dad. Everything just got to me. I told Jones that I wasn't fit but he wouldn't listen. I had to have two pain-killing jabs just to get on the pitch at all, and you know how I hate to take them. I chased Finnighan all over the park but I could never seem to catch him and he just kept on giving me lip. Then there was the crowd, and the red card, and he went and called me a "useless nigger" and something just snapped. I lost it. Simple as that."

Winston sat silent and still. Karen moved over to take Ben out of the room. Winston stopped her with a wave of his hand.

"Please Karen I hope you don't mind, but Ben should stay and listen to these things. I know he is only seven years old but he is a little brown boy and he must learn."

Karen looked over to Tony who nodded.

"You listen well Benjamin. These are important things. When I came to England many people called me a nigger. I would like to say that I did as the good Lord teaches and turned the other cheek. But I cannot say this. There were times when I did not do this. There were times when I did the same as your Daddy did and I knocked men to the ground. But I learned that it was wrong. Just because we are black we don't have the right to hit people for what they say. Now Benjamin, when some little boy calls you a nigger in the playground, and one day they will, you must not do the same thing as your Daddy. Is that right Tony?"

Tony nodded. "It's right Ben. What I did was wrong. He shouldn't have said what he said, but it was no excuse. I am ashamed of what I did. Never think it is right. Understood?"

Ben nodded. Tony took another sip of coffee. "I'm not going to mention the racism at any enquiry. It will only open a can of worms. I'll just say that he said some things and that I lost my rag. That's it. I'm not going to use it as an excuse."

Winston grinned and walloped his son on the back causing him to spit his mouthful of coffee onto the table.

"Good. That is what I was hopin' you would say. Now get your coat on and we will go."

When they got to the front door Winston said "You don't say anything to these paper men. Leave them to me."

As they walked down the path to the car the group of reporters swarmed toward them only to be stopped dead in their tracks by the roar of Winston's voice. "Get back now! Can't you see he is badly injured. Back!"

The gaggle of reporters duly obliged. "Now listen. We are on our way to a meeting with the management of the club. We will make a statement after the meeting. That's it. You've all wasted your time. Now go home. Go to church. Go."

Before any of the reporters had a chance to speak the two men jumped into the car and drove away. Tony switched on the radio and scanned until he found a local talk show.

"OK, on the line we have Stan from Kirkby, morning Stan."
"Morning."
"And what would you like to say Stan."
"I think Hobbo done right. You see what Finnighan said. He called him a nigger didn't he? I reckoned he deserved to get planted."
"We have Ollie from Ormskirk. What do you say Ollie?"
"I say the same. I mean, I know you can't just go round belting people and that, but I reckon Finnighan had it coming. I can't stand him, he's a right arrogant little . . . sorry, I can't think of what to say without swearing. But I'm with Hobbo. Us fans will stick with him, I just hope the club does the same."

As they made their way into the city centre Tony was encouraged by the fact that almost all of the calls were supportive. It would be different in the rest of the country of course, especially Manchester, but at least it looked as if his own fans were sticking by him.

When they were a mile from the ground Winston switched off the radio. "Looks like you are going to get lucky boy. Everybody seems to know what he said. If you say nothin' about it you'll come out OK."

"How come?"

Winston grinned happily. "You just leave this to me boy."

A few minutes later they walked into the Chairman's sumptuous office overlooking the pitch. Sir Robert Hyde glanced up from the papers he was working on and gave a brief smile. "Morning Tony, morning Winston. Have a seat. I'll be with you in a minute."

They sat down and Sir Robert completed reading his document and signed it. He placed in his out tray and looked up.

Bill Jones who was sitting at the side of the desk spoke immediately. "What's he doing here?"

Sir Robert raised an eyebrow. "Who?"

Jones pointed at Winston. "Him. His dad."

Sir Robert spoke slowly and calmly. "I will have you know Mr. Jones that I have been dealing with Winston from the day he brought Tony to see me as a sixteen year old YTS apprentice and I see no reason to change that now."

Winston fixed Jones with a fierce glare. "I will also point out that I am officially Tony's agent, and if you care to read his contract, you will find that clause 17 specifies that I have the right to be present at any meeting that affects the career and employment of Mr. Tony Hobbes. I assume that you are familiar with the contract Mr. Jones."

Jones was furious. Furious at the amused smirk that crossed his Chairman's face. Furious that he felt so threatened by the loud giant. All that he could think to say was. "Yeah, sure, whatever."

Sir Robert spoke in a businesslike tone. "Good. Then that's cleared up then. Gentlemen, I am afraid that we are all facing a rather difficult situation. All that matters is that we do the right thing for Liverpool Football Club. As ever, I stress that the club is bigger and more important than any of us and somehow we need to ensure that no damage is done to its reputation. Mr. Jones, I believe you have some points to raise."

Jones cleared his throat and spoke directly to the Chairman. He had no wish to try a staring contest with Winston.

"What happened yesterday was an absolute disgrace. It's impossible for me as manager to produce results on the field if my players show this kind of lack of discipline. I want to see Tony Hobbes punished for this, I want to see us give him the strongest fine that we can, in order to send a message to the other players and the FA."

Sir Robert looked to Winston who spoke carefully. "Of course we agree that a fine is entirely appropriate in this situation. Tony accepts fully that what he did was completely out of line. I believe that the clause that you will invoke in this case is number 7 in the club *Code of Behaviour* which allows a fine of up to one month's salary. We will announce to the Press today that we will voluntarily submit to a fine of two months' salary as a gesture of our grave sorrow for what has happened. We will suggest that the money for the second month will be offered to Mr. Finnighan to give to a charity of his choice."

It was hard to tell who was the most astonished at Winston's suggestion – Tony or Bill Jones. The only one who seemed to be relatively unsurprised was Sir Robert who smiled happily. "As ever Winston, I congratulate you for your wisdom. Such a press conference will do a power of good for our reputation. Consider your proposal agreed. Liverpool Football Club will match your gesture and give Mr. Finnighan our part of the fine as well. I have only one concern Winston. United. Will they play ball? I don't think that they will like the idea of our coming out of this thing looking good."

Winston smiled a big broad smile. "I think that you will have some idea of what Mr. Finnighan said to Tony. Now we will not make an issue of this unless they force us to. Now I think if you make a call to the Chairman and tell him this, I am sure that he will be happy to co-operate. After all, Manchester United Plc. would not want to see their prize asset accused of calling people niggers would they."

Sir Robert couldn't help it. He laughed. "Winston, you're a genius. I'll ring him this morning. I'll look forward to it. Now is there anything else."

Winston spoke. "There is the issue of the captaincy. We

will of course offer to resign . . . "

Sir Robert picked up the sentence straight away. ". . . and we of course will not accept it."

Jones spluttered. "Not accept it! Why that's . . . "

"Yes Mr. Jones. We will not accept it. Am I quite clear?"

Jones was livid. "Quite clear."

"Good," said Sir Robert. "Then that concludes our business."

As Jones stormed out of the room Sir Robert said "Could you stay for a moment gentlemen, there are a couple of issues that I would like to look at. Please, sit down."

They sat and Sir Robert rang for coffee.

When it had been served he spoke. "Ken Timpson called me this morning Tony. He told me that you weren't fit to play yesterday and that Jones forced you, is this true?"

"Yes."

"Why did you agree. You're no kid Tony, why did you let him bully you?"

"I don't know if I should say Sir Robert."

"Oh come on Tony, we've known each other for a long time. I hope that you realise you can be frank with me."

"OK. He threatened me with my new contract. He said that he wouldn't offer new contracts to shirkers."

Sir Robert blew out his cheeks in annoyance. "I thought as much. Now listen Tony, I have been worrying about this. I don't want to see you leave this club. You have been a great servant over the years and I would like to think that when you stop playing you will join us on the coaching side. I have a contract here ready. It is a three year extension. Now I'll be honest, it involves a 30 per cent cut in pay, but I think that is fair considering your age. All the other terms are unchanged. Please take it with you and have a look through it. If you decide to sign I would be obliged if you would keep it under your hat. Mr. Jones will not be a happy man but he will have to live with it. I would like to announce this in the summer. There's no hurry. Take your time with it."

Winston leaned over to gather up the papers. "You can be assured that we will give this our attention, although you must be aware that in the light of the Bosman ruling Tony will be able to get much better offers from elsewhere . . . "

"Give it to me Dad."

"Why?"

"Because I'm going to sign it, that's why."

"What now!"

"Yes, now."

"But you haven't even read it!"

Tony grinned at the look of utter amazement on his father's face. "I don't need to read it Dad. If Sir Robert says it is all the same except that it's 30% less, then that is good enough for me. I love this football club and have no intention of going anywhere else for a few bob extra. Now give it here."

He pulled the contract from his father's hand, put it on the desk and signed it with a flourish. He then held out his hand to Sir Robert who duly shook it.

"Pleasure doing business with you Sir."

"And you too, Tony. And you too." Sir Robert looked at his watch. "Well, I'm afraid that the next job is the press. It's a drag but it has to be done. I think that I will come and sit in on this one. I have told Mr. Jones to be in the Press room for eleven o' clock. I think we should join him."

CHAPTER THREE

Public Relations

As they walked out the Chairman's office Winston said. "We have a few minutes to spare. Give me that mobile telephone."

"Who are you ringing?" Tony asked suspiciously.

"Wait and see."

Winston pulled a small notebook from his pocket, found a number and dialled. As the phone was answered he glanced up and down the corridor to make sure that nobody was listening.

"Good morning. Is that Mrs. Finnighan? This is Winston Hobbes speakin', I'm Tony's daddy. Listen Mrs. Finnighan, I'm feelin' real bad about what my boy gone and done to your boy. I'm afraid where I come from it's always left to us parents to sort out the mess that our kids leave behind. I guess that it's the same in Ireland. It is? I thought so. Now listen, me and my boy have just had a big tellin' off from the Chairman of the club. He told Tony that they were goin' to fine him a whole month's wages but Tony is feelin' so bad about what has happened that he is going to pay *two* months of his wages. Now the Chairman has agreed that all of the money should be given to your boy to give to a charity.

"We've got to go and talk to the newspapers now, but when we're through we would like to drive over and see your boy. Tony wants to apologise in person. This thing wants calmin' down straight away. Your boy got a little excited and said some bad things about Tony's colour and Tony got even more excited and went and hit him. None of this does any good. We don't want to make an issue of the colour thing. Could you ring your boy and persuade him to see us? Good. Thank you Mrs. Finnighan. I'll call you in five minutes to make sure it is OK."

Winston snapped the phone shut and grinned with delight. Tony rolled his eyes. "Why is it that I feel that my life isn't my own any more."

His father said in a stern voice. "Because you behaved like a fool and broke a man's nose."

Brad Finnighan's mother duly informed Winston that she had persuaded her son to see them and they marched into the press conference. The room was packed. The Chairman was already inside sitting with a rather sulky looking Bill Jones. Winston and Tony joined them and Sir Robert stood up and addressed the waiting journalists.

"Good morning gentlemen. Thank you for coming at such short notice. I can inform you that Mr. Jones and I have had a meeting with Tony Hobbes and his father Winston Hobbes who acts as the player's agent. We have discussed the events of yesterday and have implemented a disciplinary procedure. I feel that it would be best if Winston Hobbes informs you of the details of this procedure as they are somewhat unusual. I can also inform you that I have spoken to the Chairman of Manchester United this morning and he has indicated his satisfaction with the measures that Liverpool Football Club has taken concerning this issue. To conclude I would like to emphasise how seriously the club is viewing this issue and how profoundly sad we are that it has happened. However I must say that I have been delighted with the response that our Club Captain has made and I feel that it should be viewed very positively.

"Winston, maybe you could say a few words."

Winston stood up to his full height and surveyed the room. When he spoke his voice boomed and the journalists flinched. "What happened yesterday was a disgraceful thing and Tony fully accepts this. There are no excuses for what he did and he is going to offer a full apology to Mr Finnighan. After this meeting me and Tony are goin' to drive to Manchester and apologise to Brad in person. You are all welcome to come with us. The rules of Liverpool Football Club allow for Tony to be fined a month's wages for what he did. Tony doesn't feel that this is enough. He is therefore payin' a fine of two months' wages. The club has agreed that the fine should be given to Brad Finnighan to give to a charity of his choice.

"Very few men go right through life without makin' a mistake. Tony has just made a very big one. He knows this and he intends to pay for it. He is upset at what he did. He can't say any more. Thank you."

The Chairman asked for questions; a forest of hands were raised.

"A question for Tony. Tony, is it the case that Brad Finnighan called you a nigger and that is why you hit him?"

Tony considered his answer carefully. "I have been a pro for seventeen years and things have always gone on, on the pitch. The difference now is that there are so many cameras taking close up shots of the players. As far as I am concerned anything that is said on the field of play is a private matter. What I will say is that there is nothing that Brad could have said to me that would have justified what I did."

"But Tony, *did* he say it?"

"I think that I have answered the question."

"Tony, don't you think that the fans have a right to know what was really said?"

Winston learned forward and spoke in a fierce voice. "Now you all listen. Brad Finnighan is one of the finest players in the game today. He had a brilliant game yesterday. Today he is in pain with a broken nose. No player deserves that. Now please will you accept that anything that he said to Tony was a private matter. Tony did wrong and he is makin' no excuses. That is the end of the matter."

It wasn't of course. The reporters made desperate efforts to get a response on the racist issue but got absolutely nowhere. The meeting was eventually brought to a close and the reporters filed out feeling that they had been cheated. When the room was finally empty Tony sank back into his chair and whistled.

Sir Robert patted him on the shoulder. "Good effort Tony. I think that things will blow over now. Just get your head down and concentrate of getting fit for the spring."

Jones looked across at Tony. "Very nicely done Hobbo.

Very nice. Well you might think that you've got away with it with the Chairman and the rest of them, but don't for a minute think that you've got away with it with me. I'm on your case Hobbo."

He stormed out of the room a very unhappy man. Tony, Winston and a gaggle of reporters headed east along the motorway to Brad Finnighan's house on the edge of Manchester. Brad's mother welcomed Winston like a long lost relative and they chatted on happily over tea. Tony and Brad were not as comfortable. They sipped their tea in silence until Tony felt that he had to say something.

"Look Brad, I was out of order. I'm sorry, OK. How's the nose?"

"Hurts like hell." Brad's voice came out slurred.

"Well let's bury the hatchet shall we?"

"We'll see."

Tony couldn't think of anything more to say. He didn't seem to be getting very far. In fact it was Finnighan who spoke. "I murdered you yesterday Hobbo. You're too slow. Your legs have gone."

"I was injured. Next time I'll be fit. Then we'll see."

"Yeah, we will."

After that they fell back into silence. When tea was finished they all headed out onto the front steps of the house and the photographers took the pictures of Brad and Tony shaking hands which would dominate the back pages of the next day's papers.

As they drove back to Liverpool Tony said. "Well I sure am glad that that's all over." He looked over to his father who was giving his full attention to the road. "Thanks Dad."

Winston grinned. "I was wonderin' when you would get round to sayin' that. Think nothin' of it, that is why you have an agent. You just do one thing for me."

"What's that."

"You go and get yourself fitter than you have ever been before, and next time you come up against that skinny, big-mouthed Irishman . . . you take him to the cleaners."

"It will be a pleasure."

CHAPTER FOUR
Africa

After the excitement of the September weekend life soon started to drag for Tony. It came as little surprise to him when he was told that his leg needed an operation. This was carried out the next week and meant that he had to suffer hobbling around in plaster for a month and a half.

He was called down to London for an FA Disciplinary committee at the end of the month. It was a painful experience. He received a nine-match ban and was fined heavily. The ban didn't really matter as his injury would keep him out for longer than that period anyway. The worst thing was that he had become branded as a complete nutter.

This new reputation caused him little harm in Liverpool. The fans by and large were delighted that he had thumped Brad Finnighan and he was fast becoming something of a cult figure. It had been a great relief to discover that his action had not caused Ben any problems at school. In fact the opposite had occurred. Having the Liverpool captain as his dad had always given Ben extra kudos with his classmates. Having the Liverpool captain who had broken Brad Finnighan's nose seemed to give him even more.

Tony decided to make the most of his enforced idleness and spend as much time as possible with his family. He had been married to Karen for ten years. She was a nurse at one of the big hospitals in the city. He had met her when he had stayed overnight with concussion after a home match against Derby.

As Tony's career had taken off Karen had shown no wish to give up her own career. Over the years she had studied hard and ground her way through a series of stiff exams. She was in line to become a Ward Sister within the next couple of years. It all made Tony feel rather guilty. He worked for three hours a day and played football on a Saturday and Tuesday night. Karen worked at least ten hours a day and often weekends as well. He felt guilty because he earned more in a fortnight than she earned in a year and he didn't work even a quarter as hard. To try and make up for this he had made the decision early on to do all he could to help out with raising Ben. He had always taken him to school in the morning and collected him in the afternoon. Unfortunately he had to stop going in the mornings when Bill Jones had insisted that training should start at 8.30.

During school holidays he had always taken Ben with him to training where the ground staff were more than happy to keep him amused whilst the players were put through their paces. Jones had told him in no uncertain terms that this was no longer allowed. He had been wondering what he would do when it was time for Ben's first half term. As it happened the problem did not arise as he was still in plaster.

Tony had been nervous when he took Ben to school the Monday morning after the Old Trafford game. He was worried about how the other parents would react. There was no need. A number of fathers came over to shake his hand and several mothers said what a wonderful gesture it had been to donate his fine to charity.

He found the same reception whenever he was out in the city. It soon became clear that nobody in Liverpool had much love for Brad Finnighan. His only real problem had come when the headmaster had called him in to inform him that Ben had been fighting. The poor man tiptoed around the issue and was obviously scared that Tony was about to thump him.

This saddened Tony. He was not a violent man and never had been. What he had done had been totally out of character but he knew that it would live with him for a long time. Some enterprising firm had printed up T-shirts with Brad Finnighan's battered face on the front along with the simple slogan: *Hobbo – Manc. Slayer.* These soon became all the rage in the city.

The plaster finally came off at the end of October and Tony was able to start very light exercise. He spent a lot of time walking and cycling and made sure that he spent at least two hours a day in the gym. Each day his leg felt a little better but he had been told not to even think of kicking a football until at least December.

It was ridiculous, but he was becoming super-fit in all the areas that didn't really matter for football. He was lifting heavier and heavier weights in the gym and he could cycle flat out for well over half an hour.

He went to watch every game home and away and it was not a happy experience. The Liverpool of Bill Jones was not a pretty side to watch. Jones had bought a lumbering six foot two striker from Bulgaria called Vladimir Chenkov and the main tactic of the team was to hoof the ball forward for him to try and head. The supporters hated this and the big Bulgarian was soon unpopular. What made things worse was that the new style was hardly successful and by the end of November the team was stuck in mid-table and twenty points behind Manchester United.

Tony often met up with one or two of the senior players for a drink after they had finished training. What he heard disturbed him. Jones was getting more and more aggressive and many of the players were becoming unsettled. He received shattering news in mid-November when Jimmy McCall rang him at home in the evening. Jimmy was a Scotsman who had been at the club for nearly as long as Tony. He was a cultured player who played on the right side of midfield. He was a clever passer of the ball and came from a long line of similar players who had graced the Anfield turf down the years.

He told Tony that Aston Villa had made him an offer and that Jones had told him to take it. Jones had told him that there was no future at the club for 'nancy boys' like him and that he should go. He was sold later in the week for £800,000 and Jones replaced him with Bill Kenyon who was bought from Rotherham in the second division.

Kenyon had the reputation of being a hard relentless midfielder and he had already collected seven yellow cards in the first few months of the season. Tony felt saddened at the way the wind was blowing at the club.

By the beginning of December the frustration was beginning to get him down. He spent a couple of hours with Ken Timpson who watched him complete a few exercises and X-Rayed his leg.

"Look Tony, things are going fine but you mustn't push it too hard. There is no way that I will let you start playing until at least February. I know that you are feeling loads better but these things take time. I have seen far too many players try to come back too soon and it can do a heap of damage. Maybe it would be different if you were 23 Tony, but you aren't. You're 33 and the older you get the longer it takes. You will only get one shot at this Tony. If you allow your leg to heal properly and take your time you can play on for at least another three years. If you push it and come back too soon it could be curtains."

Tony walked around the room impatiently. He couldn't believe it. Another two and a half months! He would go stark staring mad. "OK Ken, I can see where you are coming from. So what do I do? Just keep bashing away in the gym and on the bike?"

Timpson considered this. "No. Believe it or not, that is probably the worst thing that you can do. If you keep pushing yourself this hard you are going to do more harm than good. I think that the best thing is if you cut right down now. Just do some very light exercise and give your body time. Eat well. Take lots of vitamins and be patient. Don't flog yourself, it will only make the recovery time longer."

Tony couldn't believe it. "So what am I going to do Ken.

It's only the training that is keeping me sane. I swear, if I have to open another supermarket I'll go mad."

"Go away Tony. Take a break. School holidays are coming soon. Take the family away somewhere. Make sure that it is somewhere nice and warm. Rest and warmth. I promise you that will be the best thing."

Tony considered this. It had been ages since he had the time to take the family on a proper holiday. The demands of the long football season coupled with the demands of Karen's work made it almost impossible. He smiled. "Ken, I owe you one. That is a really good idea. To be honest what I need a break from most of all is watching the team. They aren't a pretty sight at the moment."

Timpson's face darkened. "It's a disgrace what's going on. The trouble is that there is nobody in the dressing room to stand up to him. Hopefully they will see a bit of sense soon. But I'll tell you Tony, the sooner you get back in there the better."

Tony raised the matter of the holiday later that evening when he and Karen were sitting in the lounge as Ben was watching the National Geographic channel.

"What do you think love?"

Karen pondered the question, "I think it is a marvellous idea, just what you need. I'm afraid that I am the problem. I may be able to get away for a week but they wouldn't give me any longer. You know how things are at the hospital at Christmas, it is chaos." Tony shrugged. "Well, a week it will have to be then."

"No." Said Karen. "No, that's silly. Why should I spoil things for the two of you. Why don't I come along for a week and the two of you stay on for another fortnight. I quite agree with Ken, warmth and rest will be the best thing for you Tony, and a week simply isn't enough."

Tony was appalled. "But we can't do that. That would mean that we would be away for Christmas and you would be all alone here."

She smiled. "Don't be silly Tony. I'm a big girl you know. To be honest it will be good for me to put the extra time in so that some of the younger ones can take time off. Honestly, I don't mind, and I will still have a week away. Where would you like to go? Back to Barbados again?"

"Well yes, I thought so. You know how dad feels about us keeping in touch with family. Does that suit you?"

"Of course it does. Barbados is always lovely at this time of year."

"OK then. Barbados it is."

Ben turned around from the television. "Dad."

"Yes."

"Could we go and see the animals instead?"

Tony was confused. "What animals?"

Ben pointed to the screen. It showed a herd of zebra grazing whilst two lions waited patiently in the long grass. "Those animals. The ones in Africa. Lions and elephants and hippos. Can we dad?"

Tony looked across to Karen in astonishment. Africa! He had never even dreamed of going to Africa. And yet as soon as Ben spoke the word something stirred in him. Africa. It had a kind of magic sound. He remembered his father talking to him as a boy about Africa and it occurred to him that a small part of himself was African. One day long, long ago a distant relative must have been rounded up by slavers and taken to be sold in the West Indies. And of course a small part of Ben was African too.

The more he thought the more the idea thrilled him. Ben had always adored animals and he always preferred the animal documentaries to the cartoons. They had spent many a happy afternoon down the road at the Knowlsley safari park. To see the animals in the wild would be fantastic. He looked over to Karen wondering what she would say. "Well love, what do you think?"

She laughed. "One look at your face tells me all that I need to know about what you think. I think that it is a fabulous idea. One of the nurses went to Kenya last summer. They had a sort of split holiday. They spent half the time on the beach and half the time on safari. We could do the same. I will come with you for a week on the beach and you two can go off for a fortnight's safari on your own. Now that would be smashing."

"And you really don't mind us being away for Christmas."

"Not at all. Make the most of this injury, you may never have time like this again, and Ben will certainly never be seven again. Let's do it."

Tony turned to his son. "Well partner, it looks like we are on. It will be me and you and the African bush."

Ben leapt to his feet and yelled with excitement.

Two weeks later after a long hard flight they checked into their hotel on the beach at Malindi on the coast of the Indian Ocean. It was a beautiful hotel and the white sandy beaches seemed to go on for ever. In many ways it reminded Tony a lot of Barbados but in many other ways it was very different. He was disturbed when the hotel manager told them that it was very dangerous to walk far along the beach as tourists were often beaten up and robbed. When he went into the small town he was shocked by the poverty of the houses on the outskirts that seemed to be made out of little more than cardboard.

They had a pretty good week but it was hardly peaceful. Most of the residents of the hotel were English, and many of them felt that it was fair enough for them to collar Tony and talk about football. Word soon spread among the waiters that he was Tony Hobbes, captain of Liverpool, and every morning growing gangs of children waited outside to get his autograph. He resented this a great deal less than the drunken Englishmen who wouldn't leave the family alone in the restaurant. He had never had this kind of problem in Barbados as he could always go into his father's village to escape from the other tourists. He also realised that he had become a rather more famous person since he had laid out Brad Finnighan.

At the end of the week it was time for Karen to leave. They all took a flight up to Nairobi, the capital of Kenya. At the airport they had to wait for two hours until Karen got on the flight for London.

She gave them both a hug and wished them the best of luck in the bush. For a little while Ben was a bit quiet as their bus made its way out of the city and south. Tony himself felt rather flat as he watched the landscape outside the window. It wasn't at all what he had expected. Nairobi was 5000 feet above sea level which meant that the weather was cloudy and chilly and the landscape outside was flat and boring. There were no animals to be seen, just fields of crops and cattle and the occasional downbeat town.

However as they drove south they started to lose altitude and the landscape changed. Ben fell asleep for three hours and when he woke up everything was different. The country was drier and more like he had seen on the television. Eventually they passed a sign that informed them that they were entering the Amboseli game reserve and Ben became excited as he started to see more and more animals through the window of the bus.

They had booked onto a two week safari which would

take them around several of the best game parks in Kenya, starting with Amboseli. Each game park boasted a superb luxury lodge to stay in and special Land Rovers to take them out into the bush.

The first three days were wonderful. Amboseli was a truly beautiful place to be, especially in the early morning. They got up a little after five and joined the first safari of the day. It was the perfect time to be out. As the big sun climbed into the sky it coloured the snow on the top of the massive Mount Kilimanjaro an amazing red and orange. Dawn was the time when the animals would come to the waterholes to drink, and in three days they saw nearly all the animals that Ben had longed for.

By the end of each day Ben was tired out with all the excitement and fresh air and he would be fast asleep by seven o' clock.

After three days at Amboseli they got on to the bus and headed south for Tsavo. This was a different game park altogether. It was absolutely massive and stretched for the same distance as Liverpool to London. It was much drier than Amboseli and more like a desert. Tony felt a tremendous surging feeling as they went for mile after mile down the dusty tracks of the park seeing absolutely nobody.

This he felt was the real Africa; a hard, beautiful empty place. It thrilled him. He felt rather differently about where they were staying. Another beautiful lodge in the small village of Voi. It was luxuriously comfortable but somehow it didn't feel right. Every time they drove through another poor dusty village Tony felt more and more awkward about staying in such luxury. He also felt that he was missing something. He was keen to see Africa but he was only seeing a very small part of it. At times he felt as if he was in a cinema, looking out from air conditioned luxury. It bothered him greatly that he didn't seem to be meeting any Africans and he really wasn't learning anything about how they lived.

Once again the tourists were beginning to get on his nerves. He never seemed to get a moment's peace as they pestered him constantly. Their third day in Tsavo was a Saturday. They had been out all afternoon on a game run and Ben was tired out. Tony had taken him to his room for a nap and he had decided to have a wander about. He suddenly remembered the time difference. 5.30 in Kenya was 3.30 in England. He chuckled as he realised that he had quite forgotten that Liverpool were playing away at Everton at that very minute.

There was already half an hour gone. How on earth could he find out the score? He saw one of the drivers working on the engine of his Land Rover at the edge of the car park. He was called Thomas and he had often talked to Tony about football as they had driven around. Tony walked across to where he was tinkering with the engine.

"Hi Thomas."

Thomas pulled himself out of the engine and beamed as he wiped his oily hands on a piece of rag. "Hello Mr. Tony. How are you?"

"Oh fine, but I could do with a bit of help."

"If it is possible for me to be of an assistance Mr. Tony, it would make me very happy."

"Do you have a radio?"

"Yes Mr. Tony. A radio is something that I have."

"Great. Now listen Thomas. Liverpool are playing at Everton this afternoon and I would really like to listen to it on the *World Service.*" Thomas beamed even wider. "Of course you will want to hear this. I know that it is a very important game. I believe it is what you call a Derby match."

"Bang right Thomas. So could you come round to my room with it. I'd come with you but I can't leave Ben, he's asleep you see."

"But of course Mr. Tony. I will be there in no longer time than ten minutes. But tell me just one thing. Why is it that they call this game a Derby?"

Tony laughed. "To be honest Thomas, I have often wondered the same thing myself. I'm afraid that I haven't got a clue!"

Thomas was true to his word and turned up with his radio ten minutes later. They were in time for the second half. It was 0–0 but Everton were piling on the pressure. After sixty minutes Tony groaned as the crackly little radio seemed to burst with sound as Everton scored from a corner. Liverpool made efforts to get back into the game but they never really created any chances. At last the whistle blew and the commentator talked a bit about the crisis at Liverpool. The defeat had taken them down to seventeenth in the table and there were suggestions that relegation could become a possibility.

Worse was to come. The next report told of how Manchester United had put on a magical display to win 4–2 away at Newcastle. Brad Finnighan had scored two. Tony switched off the radio in annoyance.

Thomas looked heavily serious. "It is indeed a very poor result Mr. Tony. I feel that the team must be feeling your loss."

"Well thanks for your confidence Thomas, but there is more than me being out that is wrong with Liverpool at the moment, our new manager . . . "

He was interrupted by a man in a suit who had walked

up to the veranda where they were sitting. He was one of the under managers from the hotel's reception area.

"Excuse me Mr. Hobbes, but is this man bothering you?"

Tony was amazed. "No. Of course he isn't. He has kindly brought me a radio to listen to the football commentary. Why do you ask?"

"Sorry sir. Staff boys are not allowed to go to tourists' rooms. It is a rule of the hotel. It is best if he goes now."

"Best for who?" Tony was starting to get angry.

Thomas spoke quietly so that the manager could not hear him. "Please do not upset him Mr. Tony. It will be bad for me." Then in a louder voice. "Thank you Mr. Tony. I will go now.

He picked up his radio and left.

Ben woke up a few minutes later and Tony took him across the car park to where Thomas was once again working on his engine.

"I hope that you won't be in any trouble Thomas, I had no idea. If there is anything that I can do to help just say."

Thomas smiled. "No Mr. Tony. Thank you, but there is no need. I have some difficulty with these people here."

Tony was confused. "Why?"

"Because I am not from here Mr. Tony. My home is Uganda. There is no work for me in my own country so I have to come here. These boss men are all Kikuyu people. Kikuyu men not like Ugandans. It can be hard."

This saddened Tony. The only racism that he had ever known was white against black. It seemed almost worse when it was black against black. "I'm sorry to hear this Thomas. Maybe you could help me again. There is one thing that is disappointing me about my trip here. I never really seem to meet any African people. Where do you go on a Saturday night? Maybe you could take us with you?

I'll square it with the manager first of course."

Once again Thomas grinned hugely. "This I can do Mr. Tony. I go to a small bar in the village of Voi. You will like it. They cook very good chicken and play good music. Many people go there. Kikuyu, Masai, Tanzanian, Ugandan, many. You will like it there."

"Then we're on. What time ?"

"I will pick you up at seven o' clock."

CHAPTER FIVE

Uganda

As soon as Tony and Ben walked into the restaurant with Thomas that evening he knew that he was going to like it. The name which was hand painted onto an old piece of timber by the door made him smile. It was called *The Great Western Eating House*. It was hard to see where the *Great* came from but it certainly reminded him of a Western. The big shack seemed to be entirely built from rusty pieces of corrugated iron and it was more or less held together with string.

What was certain was that it was popular. Loud African music beat hard and every table seemed to be full. A big bald man in an apron waved to Thomas as they walked in. He led them to a small table in the middle of the room and beamed at Tony. "For very famous man we reserve table, Mr. Tony Hobbes."

They ate chicken and corn cakes and drank several bottles of the local beer. The owner had three sons and they took Ben out into the dusty back yard to play football. There were soon many men crowded around the table asking Tony question after question about his life in England. Although this was far more hassle than he would have had in the hotel he didn't mind in the slightest. He just felt happy at last to be meeting some African people.

Time flew by and he was amazed when he looked at his watch and discovered that it was after eleven. He started to make his farewells and half an hour later he carried his sleepy son to the Land Rover.

When they got in he said, "Thanks for that Thomas. We've had a great time. We have just over a week left here and I would like to do more of this. How do you suggest that we go about it?"

Thomas stared out of the window thoughtfully. "Maybe I could help Mr. Tony."

"Go on."

"My Christmas holiday is starting tomorrow. I am going home to see my family in Uganda. It is a very long journey. Many buses. If you want I can take you. These many buses would be too hard for the little boy. But if you hired a car the journey would not be so long. We could both drive. On the way I show you many beautiful places. When we get there you like my country very much. White men called my country 'The Pearl of Africa' because it is so beautiful.

My village is in the East of Uganda, near to the mountains. You have never seen such mountains Mr. Tony. They are called the Mountains of the Moon."

Tony was staggered by the offer. "Wow. That sounds absolutely brilliant. My only worry is little Ben. You see, we came here to see animals."

Thomas grinned. "You no worry Mr. Tony. My brother Samuel he is working as a warden in the National Park. It is called the Ruwenzori. There are very big forests there. He will take us there. He will show you the gorillas. There is no greater thing to see. This I make promise to you."

That was enough to make up Tony's mind. The next morning was busy as he made arrangements. The tour leader was horrified to hear that his famous guest was leaving. Tony gave few details and never let anyone know where he was going in case it gave Thomas trouble when he returned to the hotel after Christmas. A little before lunchtime a hire company delivered a big Toyota 4 X 4 and Tony was off. He collected Thomas from the restaurant and they headed north.

Their journey took them three days but it was filled with magic. They passed the massive snowy peak of Mount Kenya. They saw the millions of pink flamingos on lake Nakuru. They saw the small stream that was the source of the river Nile as it trickled out of Lake Victoria. They stopped at the airport in Kampala, the capital of Uganda, and Tony altered his flight home.

As they drove east for mile after mile Tony could only agree with Thomas. It was indeed a beautiful country. The towns and villages were run down and very poor but the people were more friendly than any he had ever met before. As they drove Thomas told him all about the village. His father was the local chief and so had to deal with all aspects of the life of the community. After two days Tony felt that he already knew many of the people as Thomas told tale after tale of the life of the village.

It was just after lunchtime on the third day when Thomas stopped the car and pointed to a cluster of thatched huts on top of a small hill. "This Mapote. This is my home."

As they parked up in the middle of the village, children seemed to appear from nowhere and they danced around the vehicle. A tall, grave looking man came out of a hut that was rather bigger than the rest. His stern expression vanished as soon as he saw Thomas and he grinned.

Thomas said to Tony. "This is my father. He is our chief."

The rest of that day and the whole of the next day were endlessly busy. Thomas introduced Tony to everyone and took him around the coffee plantations that gave the people their living. Samuel, Thomas's brother arrived in the evening and agreed to take them to see the gorillas the next day. Tony smiled when he realised that the next day was Christmas Day. What a very odd way to spend Christmas.

They were up well before dawn and they drove for four hours along small bumpy tracks which climbed higher and higher into the mountains. As they drove, the forests of huge trees closed around them tighter and tighter. Every now and then they would reach a pass and the view would open up before them. Tony gasped at the astonishing scenery as the seemingly unending forests swept up to jagged snowy peaks.

At last they stopped at a small clearing with two huts. Samuel took them inside and told them that this was his home and his office. He made them tea and cooked eggs. A little after nine they started out and walked into the forest.

They walked and walked and walked. It was tough going

as they had to clamber over roots and duck under vines. They stopped for five minutes every hour and drank tea from a flask. During the third halt Samuel tapped Tony on the shoulder and pointed to Ben. Ben had a look of complete wonder on his face and he was listening to the weird collection of bird sounds that echoed around the trees.

"Mr. Tony. This boy is a young lion. For three hours we are walking very hard but he no complain. He is strong boy. You are proud father I think."

Tony looked at his son fondly. "Very proud."

"I think too that your leg must be feeling better now."

Tony was amazed. He hadn't even thought about his leg for days. Samuel was right. He had marched away for three hours and it didn't even ache. Now that was a good Christmas present.

Samuel became serious. "Now you must listen to me good Mr. Tony. Very soon we will come to the gorillas. They are good animals and they will do us no harm. They will only attack us if we make them frightened. When we get there the big male silverback will come and look at us. You must not move Mr. Tony. You just stand very still and he will accept us."

After they had walked a further ten minutes they heard a tremendous crashing sound. It was the sound of big branches splitting. Samuel put his hand up and they walked very slowly.

And suddenly they were there. There were five of them. A huge silverback male, two smaller females and two babies. The silverback was simply enormous. Tony guessed that he must have weighed nearly a hundred stone. He snapped a big thick branch off a tree and Tony could not believe his strength. As he munched away at the leaves on the branch he glanced over to them. Eventually he put down the branch and seemed mildly annoyed at having guests. He loped across to where they stood and sat down on a tree stump no more than six feet away.

Tony knew that he had never been half as frightened in his whole life. He tightened his grip on Ben's shoulder. Samuel spoke very softly. "It is OK. He just wants to see who we are. Just stand very still. You need not have fear Mr. Ben."

When Ben spoke back his voice was quite normal. "I'm not frightened Sam". Tony didn't think that he could speak at all.

The silverback scratched and fidgeted for five minutes and then got bored with them and went and sat down with his branch. He grunted to the two females who gave their visitors a quick look and then ignored them.

They stayed with the gorillas for over an hour and one of the babies even came over and felt Ben's hair. Its mother was not amused and soon dragged it away by the scruff of its neck.

As they made their way back to Samuel's hut Tony felt more exhilarated than he had ever felt before. To his amazement he realised that being handed the FA cup at Wembley was nothing compared to what he had just experienced.

As they drove back out of the mountains Ben fell fast asleep. Tony's fantastic mood was spoilt as Samuel told him of the terrible dangers that the gorillas faced from poachers. The wardens did what they could, but the forests were so huge that it was impossible to keep the poachers away. If it continued, then the gorillas would soon die out.

When they arrived back at the village Ben didn't wake up as Tony lifted him out of the Toyota and carried him into the hut that they had been given. As he walked over to the Chief's hut he limped very slightly as his leg was starting to stiffen.

Christmas dinner was corn cakes, monkey meat and beer. Somewhere far away Liverpool were due to play away at West Ham the next day, but it seemed so far away as not to be real any more.

Tony soon found that his own eyes were growing heavy in the warm smoky hut. He stood up and started to say goodnight to everyone. The chief gave Thomas a look and nodded to him.

Thomas cleared his throat and spoke very formally. "Mr. Tony. My father he ask me to speak for him. He ask me to beg from you very big favour. Is it good that I should speak."

"Of course" said Tony and sat down again, feeling slightly uneasy. Thomas continued.

"Tomorrow he is Boxing Day. It is a day when we have a tradition here in Mapote. Our next village is Misumba, over this way." Thomas pointed in a northerly direction. "On every Boxing Day there is a football match between the men of Mapote and the men of Misumba. Tony, my chief says that you are now a man of Mapote. He says you should play this game with the other men of Mapote. He says this is a good thing. He says it is a good thing because for many, many years the men of Mapote they never can win this game."

It was a tough decision. If he made his injury worse by playing in a game in the middle of Africa there would be real trouble. But then it occurred to Tony that if he did in fact make his leg worse there was absolutely no way that anyone at the club would ever know how it had happened. It was a big advantage to be so far in the middle of

47

nowhere. These people had been wonderful to him and to Ben. The least that he could do was to play football with them. He was quite confident about his leg. It had stood up to the long hike in the jungle really well. It was time that he kicked a ball anyway.

"No problem Thomas. But listen, my leg is not right yet. I'll have to play in defence. Deep at the back. I can't afford to run around too much. If you'll take me as a defender then I'm with you."

The hut erupted with cheers at the news. As Tony made his way back to his own hut he realised that this was a big game for his new friends.

CHAPTER SIX

Boxing Day in Mizumba

The next day the whole village walked for two miles through the coffee plantations to the village of Misumba. It was clear to Tony that Misumba was a much larger village than Mapote. There was a real carnival atmosphere about the place. The whole population of the village had gathered around a small flat field which was marked out as a pitch. There where two sets of goalposts which were made from bamboo and roughly tied up with rope.

The people of Misumba were gathered along the far touchline. The air was filled with the smell of cooking as a pig was being roasted over an open fire. There were several drums and small boys beat out a throbbing rhythm. The Mapote villagers settled themselves down on the opposite touchline and some of the boys unstrapped the drums that they carried on their backs and started to beat them. Both sides competed in singing and dancing.

A very old Land Rover pulled up and a silver-haired white man got out. He was quite old and tanned, dark from years in the African sun. He wore the collar of a priest.

He smiled warmly as he came over to the Chief and Tony. "Good morning to you Mr. Hobbes. To be sure news travels fast in these parts. It would seem that Mapote may make a bit more of a game of it this year. I hope so. Misumba won 13–0 last year. Let me introduce myself. I'm Father O'Malley. I'm a missionary and they always get me to be the referee. I can't keep up with play as well as I once could but I like to think that the Good Lord helps me with my decisions."

He had a warm Irish voice and Tony liked him straight away. As the two teams made their way out onto the pitch Tony could see why Mapote had not won for so long. His team was a real mixture of old and young. Three of his fellow defenders must have been well into their fifties and two of the midfield could not have been much older than twelve.

This certainly was not the case with the Misumba team. The larger village certainly had a larger squad of players to chose from and most of their players seemed to be very fit looking young men in their twenties.

His fears were more than borne out when the game started. The younger men of Misumba poured down on the ageing Mapote defence. Any hopes that Tony had of an easy morning stroll soon vanished. He was soon breathing hard as he had to throw himself into tackle after tackle to try to stop the constant Misumba attacks. He couldn't remember having to work so hard. His fellow players gave it absolutely everything but after twenty minutes their defence was at last broken and Misumba scored.

Every now and then when the ball flew over the bar and into the coffee bushes there was a chance to take a breather whilst the little boys raced to collect the ball. On these occasions Tony looked over to the touchline to check that Ben was OK. He saw that he was with a tall thin boy who was much paler than the other villagers. He hadn't seen him before.

Ben had brought his football with him and he was laughing with delight as his new friend performed a series of tricks. After two more goals the ball once again was hoofed deep into the coffee and Tony once again watched the pale boy. He was tremendously clever with the ball, and he effortlessly juggled it from foot to foot, onto his head, onto the back of his neck, back to his foot. Tony couldn't help but whistle to himself as the boy kicked the ball high in the air, did a cartwheel, and collected it easily on his chest as it dropped.

At long last the half time whistle was blown and the weary men of Mapote trudged back to their supporters whilst the Misumba team were greeted by drums and singing.

Tony wandered over to Ben. "You OK Ben?"

"I'm great Dad. This is my new friend Simon."

Tony shook the boy's hand. The boy said very formally. "It is a very big honour to meet you Mr. Tony Hobbes. My name is Simon Matembo."

"Who are you supporting then Simon. Are you a Misumba man."

"No Sir. I am here to support Mapote. I am of Mapote."

"That's strange," said Tony. "We have never seen you in the village."

"No. This is true." The boy seemed uneasy. There was something strange about him. His skin was so much lighter than any of the other villagers and the shape of his face was different too. Tony was curious. "Why is that Simon?"

"It is how it must be sir. Me and my mother live some distance from the village. We live a private life."

"Well why are you not playing Simon, you seem pretty skilful, I reckon that we could do with you. What is the problem? Do you not like playing in actual games?"

Simon's eyes flashed. "Why no sir. I love football. Football is my life."

Stranger and stranger. "Then why?" Asked Tony.

"Because it is best," said the boy rather sadly.

At this point Father O'Malley came over. "Well Tony, uphill battle wouldn't you say?"

"Just a bit," said Tony. "I'm just trying to persuade young Simon here to join us. He looks like he could give us another striking option. The priest's face darkened and he led Tony to one side.

"I'd be careful Tony. You may open up a can of worms here. The Mapote men won't let Simon play."

"Why on earth not?"

O'Malley sighed. "Look Tony, it's a very long story. I'll tell it quickly. Years ago there was a young missionary from England in Mapote. One day he found a young girl who had walked from the mountains. The poor thing was half dead from starvation and he took her in. She recovered but the villagers were never happy. They said that she was a witch. She grew up at the mission house and he educated her. She grew into a beautiful young thing and then things went wrong. She became pregnant and the missionary fled back to England. That is why Simon is such a light colour. The missionary was the father. His mother went to live in a hut about a mile from the village. The villagers don't dare drive her away. They are frightened that she would put a curse on them. But they have nothing to do with either her or her son."

Tony felt angry. "Come on Father, this is hocus pocus. I'm not having this."

"Be careful Tony."

"Careful nothing. Simon, come with me."

He marched over to where the other members of the team were catching their breath for the second half. "Thomas. It is time for a substitution. I've been watching this lad. I reckon he is just what we need up front."

Thomas looked appalled. "Mr. Tony. Please, this is not a good thing. This boy he is not to play." The chief spoke fast to his son. Thomas translated. "Chief he say no. He say boy is no play. This must be Mr. Tony."

Tony was livid. "Now you tell the chief this. If he has a problem because Simon here has a white daddy and a black mummy, then he has another problem. You see I have a black daddy and a white mummy. So if Simon can't play for Mapote, then neither can I."

This caused an outpouring of conversation. At last the chief, who was hugely troubled, gave his reluctant permission. Tony was delighted. He clapped Simon on the back. "OK my friend you're on. If you are as good on the pitch as you are at doing tricks we are still in this game."

The boy seemed both delighted and nervous.

O'Malley blew his whistle and they made their way back onto the pitch. There was a change in the mood when the Misumba supporters saw Simon line up in attack. The game started and it was more fast and furious than before. Tony saw that Simon was constantly being kicked and pushed when the referee was looking the other way. The worst culprit was a huge man who played in the Misumba defence.

When Misumba won a corner Tony decided to take some action. At the moment that the big defender jumped, Tony nudged him hard in the back with his shoulder and sent him crashing to the floor. The big man leapt to his feet and eye-balled Tony. Tony pushed his face in close. "Listen big man, you leave the kid alone or I'll have you, got that!"

O'Malley pulled them apart and tutted at Tony. Ten minutes into the second half Tony won the ball with a thumping tackle and looked up. He clipped a high ball forward for Simon to run on to. The boy collected the pass on his chest without slowing his run. He then nudged the ball over a defender's head with his right thigh and smashed the ball as it dropped, with his left foot. The ball had never hit the ground and the boy had never broken his stride. The ball shot into the corner of the goal like a bullet. It was without doubt the finest piece of sheer skill that Tony had ever seen. The goal was met by total silence either side of the pitch. Tony ran forward to congratulate Simon who was smiling happily. "Great goal son. Keep it going."

The other players completely ignored him. The pace of the game intensified. Simon was kicked time and time again, and Tony found that he was playing harder and harder. Four more times he managed to find enough space in the wild pace of the match to hit telling through balls to Simon. On each occasion the boy scored with skill that was absolutely breathtaking.

At last O'Malley blew his whistle. Mapote had won 5–4. Yet there were no celebrations. Both sets of supporters simply packed up and made their way home. Thomas seemed guilty when he came over to Tony.

"Thank you Mr. Tony. You played a fine game. My people should thank you as well. I am sorry that they are so rude."

"It's not me that they should thank," said Tony. "It is young Simon. He won you the game."

Thomas shook his head. "He does not play real football. He is playing the devil's football. It was the bad spirits of the forest who were playing there Mr. Tony."

"I'm sorry Thomas but I cannot believe that."

Thomas smiled sadly. "You must believe what you believe Mr. Tony. I will go now."

O'Malley came over. "Well Tony you've made it a day to remember. Can I give you a lift?"

"No thanks father. I'll walk the boy home. He looks like he needs some company." He looked over sadly to where Simon was sitting talking to Ben.

O'Malley smiled at him. "This is Africa Tony. There are many things that seem strange to us. At times we have tried to interfere when we maybe should have left things well alone. I have been here for forty years, and I can promise you that there is nothing that you can do."

Tony looked at him evenly. "Ah but there is Father O'Malley, there is. You see, I believe that I have just played on the same pitch as one of the greatest talents on the planet. I'm not talking pretty good here. I'm talking *Pele* and Maradonna. Now I may not know much about African culture but I do know about football. I'm taking the boy away from here O'Malley. He is going to pull on a Liverpool shirt and get what he deserves. And God help anyone who tries to stop me."

CHAPTER SEVEN

Persuasion

Tony and Simon talked together quietly as they made their way back through the coffee plantations to Mapote. When they were about a quarter of a mile from the village they turned onto a small path which wound its way up the side of a hill. After a few hundred yards they came to the top where a single hut stood looking down on the plantations below.

The hut was neat and well maintained and it was surrounded by a colourful garden of flowers. At one side of the hut there was a large vegetable garden where a young woman was working at pulling up weeds. She sang softly to herself as she worked, and the sound of her voice coupled with the light breeze which was rustling the trees gave Tony a huge sense of tranquillity.

She turned and smiled as Simon spoke to her.

"Mother, please allow me to introduce you to my new friends. This is Mr. Tony and his son Mr. Ben. They are here visiting Mapote. They are from England."

She wiped the dusty soil from her hands and smiled warmly as she greeted them. Tony was knocked back by her beauty, which was spectacular. She seemed to be little more than 35 years old which meant that she must have been very young when she had given birth to Simon.

She pulled up some home made stools and they sat in front of the hut whilst a pot of water came to the boil. Tony was very impressed by the dazzling array of flowers which grew all around him.

"I must congratulate you on your garden Mrs. Matembo, it is truly beautiful."

"Why thank you, gardening has always been a passion for me. Now please, you must both call me Rose, you see, I am even named after a flower."

"Also, I must say that your English is exceptional. I was wondering how it was that Simon spoke the language so well, now I can see why."

Her eyes became slightly sad and distant. "Well, I had a very good teacher, but that was a long, long time ago. I'm glad to know that it has stood the test of time."

She made coffee and they talked. Tony was impressed at the way that she brought Ben into the conversation and listened to him carefully. It was in fact Ben who described the match with Misumba, which he did which great relish. Tony smiled as his desperate exploits in the centre of the Mapote defence paled into insignificance when compared to Simon's spectacular goals. Rose was delighted and said,

"I'm so pleased. Simon spends hours and hours with

his football, it is so nice that he has been able to play in a real game."

She prepared lunch and told them a little of their life at the top of the hill. She showed an amazing lack of bitterness towards the villagers who had excluded her and her son. They lived a very simple, quiet life.

When lunch was finished Tony asked Simon if he would take Ben for a look round. Simon agreed readily and the two boys went away. Tony took a deep breath and decided to begin. He knew that what he was about to do was going to be tough.

"Tell me Rose, how much do you know about football?"

She shook her head. "Very little I'm afraid. As you can guess, we are isolated here. We know little of what goes on in the outside world. Tell me please, it is of interest."

Tony explained about the massive explosion of interest in football, from all over the world. He told of World Cups and massive shiny stadiums packed with supporters. He told of the newspapers and the television and the new supporters' megastores.

At times her mouth opened in wonder when he told her of the price of tickets or replica shirts.

She nearly fell off her stool when he told her of how much he earned as a Liverpool player. This made her thoughtful. "Tell me Mr. Tony. Can this be right? Can it be right for a man to earn such riches for playing a game when there are so many who are hungry?"

Tony shook his head. "Since I have been in Uganda I have thought of little else Rose. What can I say? Of course it is not right, but then there is an awful lot that is wrong with the world."

They were silent for a while. At last she spoke. "Mr. Tony there is something that you want to say to me but you lack the courage. Please do not be afraid. I am but a poor woman and I will do you no harm. The people of Mapote credit me with all sorts of powers but, alas, I do not possess them."

Tony took a deep breath. "Rose, I have been a professional footballer since I was 16 years old. That is seventeen years. I have played my game at the very highest level. I have played in the World Cup finals and I have been lucky enough to play against the best players on earth." He paused and chose his words with care. "However I saw the greatest of them all playing this morning in Misumba. Your son is not simply a good footballer, he is exceptional, one in ten million. His talent is greater than anything that I have ever seen. I would like to take him to England so that he can use his talent to the full.

'I could tell you of the fame that he will know and the vast sums of money that he will earn, but these things are not what is most important. What is most important is that such an exceptional talent should not be wasted."

She sighed as he spoke these words. "Of course you are right Mr. Tony. Simon is now nearly a man. I have always known that the time must come when he must leave me. It is hard for any mother, maybe you can see that it is particularly hard for me. But I would never stand in his way. But you must tell me more. Where will he live? How will he eat? Where will he find the warm clothes that he will need in such a cold country?"

"He will stay with me. I have a wife called Karen and I promise that we will be like mother and father to him. I guarantee that I would never allow any harm to come to Simon any more than I would allow it to come to Ben."

She looked deep into his face and was very quiet. "I see that this is true. I feel that you are a good man Mr. Tony. I feel that I may trust you with my son. I will show you something."

She disappeared into the hut for a few minutes and then came out with two envelopes. "Do you know anything of my history, Mr. Tony?"

"A little, Father O'Malley told me some."

"He is a good man. He visits me sometimes. He will have told you that it was a fellow missionary who is Simon's father. He was a good man too. I loved him. When he found that I was pregnant he could not bear the shame and he ran away. I do not blame him for this for he was only young. Sometimes we receive letters from him. He is now a priest in a place called Halifax. Sometimes he sends money, twice he has sent these."

She passed the two envelopes to Tony. Inside were two British passports both made out in the name of Simon Matembo. She continued. "He sent the first one a year after he left this place. The second one came ten years later when the first expired. I believe that one of your worries must have been a passport. Well as you can see, you have no need to worry after all."

Again she paused and gazed sadly over the endless green hills. "You may take my son Mr. Tony. He is lucky to have found a man like you."

Simon and Ben joined them a few minutes later and Ben rattled on happily about some birds that they had seen on their walk.

When Ben had finished Rose said to her son. "Simon. Mr. Tony has something to say to you and you must listen carefully. He has talked to me about this thing and I agree with what he says."

Simon looked at Tony with interest. Tony started his speech. "Simon, I have seen many, many footballers in my life, but none of them are as good as you. God has given you a great talent. I would like you to come with me and Ben to England. You will live with us in our home. I will take you to play for my club, Liverpool. I will help you become one of the greatest players in the world. I promise that I will always be with you. You will never be alone."

Ben leapt off his stool and shrieked with joy. "Oh Simon, this is great, you will have the room next to mine, and I will show you my computer and my bike and everything."

But Simon did not leap for joy. His big eyes filled with tears and he fought hard not to let them fall. "Mr. Tony, you are very kind, but I must say no. I told you that football is my life. This is nearly true, but it is not my life. I would love more than anything to come with you to England. But I cannot. I cannot leave my mother alone with these people who say that she is a witch. I have spoken now. It must not be."

Both Rose and Tony tried to change his mind but neither was able to. At last he stood up from the stool and spoke to his mother. "Mother, I am 17 years old. I am a man now. You can not tell me what to do. I will not leave."

He started to walk away very slowly. Tony shouted after him. "Simon, I will sort things out. I promise. I will be back soon."

The boy never turned his head as he walked away.

Four days later they were back home in Liverpool. Karen's eyes were wide as Ben recounted their many adventures. She kept looking over to Tony with a questioning look on her face. On each occasion he gave a small smile and nodded. Later, when Ben at last ran out of steam and went to bed Tony and Karen sat together in the lounge. She leaned her head on his shoulder and said. "I go to Africa and we have a simple week on the beach, and then as soon as the pair of you are out of my sight, well, I can barely believe it. What adventures!"

He chuckled. "What adventures indeed. We certainly had a fair old time."

"Tell me about Simon."

He told her and tried to put into words the magic of the young man's ability. He tried to explain the impact that Africa had made on him and how he had to find a way to help the gifted young Ugandan."

She thought about what he said. "So you will be going back?"

"I must."

"But what else can you say? What can make him change his mind? Should you change his mind? After all, think how it would be for his mother."

He groaned. "I know, I know, I know. I thought of nothing else all the way home on the plane. I don't know what to do, but I have to do something."

She brightened. "Well I know what you have to do and I am amazed that it hasn't occurred to you."

"What?"

"You need to talk to your dad. If anyone can sort this out, then my guess is that it is Winston."

A slow smile spread over Tony's face. "You're absolutely right. Of course. Dad will know what to do."

He drove round to his father's house the next evening. To start with Winston was delighted to hear that his son had left the official tour and had gone to find the real Africa. He was fascinated to hear about the Boxing Day match but became suspicious when Tony said that he needed his help. When Tony said that he was going back to try and bring Simon over he was appalled.

"Boy, you've gone clean out of your head. How can you

say that this boy is that good? This is madness."

"Dad, have I ever given you a lecture on Union Law?"

"Of course not."

"Then please do not try to tell me about football. I tell you, Simon is a world beater, you just have to believe me."

Winston grunted. "Well I accept that. So what help do you want from me?"

"Come with me when I go back. You'll work something out. You know what these villages are like, it is like Barbados."

The big man nearly exploded. "Boy you are crazy. I don't have some easy, lazy job like you! I can't just go swannin' off to Africa to persuade some young boy to be a footballer! I'm just a simple dock worker, I can't go payin' no fancy air fares."

"Come on dad, you haven't taken a holiday in years and I'm paying. Come on man, show some spirit."

The argument raged for two hours more, but after half an hour Tony knew that he had hooked his prey. When at last he agreed to join Tony in a return trip, his father started to grill him mercilessly about every aspect of life in the village of Mapone.

A little after midnight he told his son of his plan. By one in the morning the plan was agreed. Three weeks later they sat next to each other as their plane touched down at Jinja airport on the outskirts of Kampala.

CHAPTER EIGHT

The Big Chief of the Mersey

Winston and Tony spent a busy day and a half shopping in Kampala and they made several more stops on the road east to Mapote. Tony was amazed at the ease with which his father dropped into the rhythm of African life. Within a matter of minutes the big man dominated every market place or restaurant that they visited.

When they were about five miles from Mapote they stopped the small lorry that they had hired and Winston got changed. His jeans and sweatshirt were packed away. He replaced them with a long white robe which he tied around his waist with a bright red sash. He hung a large gold chain around his neck. He grinned at Tony. "Well boy, how do I look?"

"Like a dog's dinner, to be honest."

Tony had been far from convinced about the outfit that his father had insisted on wearing, but Winston had said that it was vital that he made a big impression. As he looked his father up and down he couldn't help but agree that he would definitely make an impression. His father tapped his head comically and said. "I nearly forgot. There is one more item."

He rummaged in his bag and pulled out a thick varnished walking stick with a flourish. Tony groaned.

Twenty minutes later Tony parked the truck in front of the Chief's hut. The villagers poured out to see who had come to visit. Several grinned happily when they recognised Tony. They all gasped in astonishment as Winston slowly stepped out of the passenger door. Tony was both delighted and relieved when he saw Thomas's brother Samuel, come out from his father's hut. Without Samuel, finding a translator would have been difficult.

Winston stood up to his full six and a half feet and said in a commanding voice. "Show me where I can find the chief of this place. Tell him that I have been sent from far away. Tell him that I come from The Big Chief of the Mersey himself. Tell him that the Big Chief of the Mersey sends him messages and gifts."

Samuel's eyes nearly popped out and he scuttled back into the hut to fetch his father. When the Chief came out Winston gave him an elaborate bow and again spoke in a loud voice.

"I bring you greetings from the Great Chief of the Mersey. This is a Chief who is so great that beside him I am as small as a mouse."

The watching crowd gasped as Samuel translated. Any man who made the giant in the white robe look as small as a mouse must be a great man indeed. Winston continued. "My boy here has told my Chief all about the great people of Mapote. He has told of many things. My Chief has sent me with many messages. But before I give these messages he has ordered me to bring a great feast. Tony, open the back of the truck."

Tony, who was finding it terribly difficult to keep a straight face, opened the back of the truck. Inside were chickens, three pigs, many crates of beer, and a whole host of other foods that they had bought in Kampala. A cheer went up from the villagers when they saw the contents of the truck and within minutes they had started to prepare the feast.

Whilst fires were lit and tables were pulled out, Winston and Tony sat with Samuel and the Chief in front of the hut. Winston sat bolt upright on his stool with his hands laid one over the other on his stick. He said little, he merely watched the preparations being made in front of him with a face like stone. Young children crept up to look at him more closely, and one was even brave enough to reach out and touch his stick. Winston never moved a muscle.

Three hours later darkness had fallen and the huge banquet was prepared. The Chief rose to his feet and waved for silence. Samuel translated for Winston and Tony.

"We welcome our visitors. We welcome Mr. Tony and his father, the representative of The Great Chief of the Mersey. We thank this Great Chief for the feast he has brought. We will listen to his message."

The Chief sat and Winston slowly drew himself up to his full height. He paused for a long moment, then started his speech.

"My Chief is a very great man. He rules a very great kingdom. His kingdom is called Liverpool. It sits on the mighty river Mersey and it is far, far away. My Chief has listened to my son Tony. My son Tony came back from Mapote and he told my Chief many things. But it is only one thing that made my Chief send me all this way to see you."

Again a long, long pause. The tension was electric.

"Tony told my Chief about a boy called Simon Matembo. He said that this boy was a great footballer. For my Chief, football is more important than all other things. My Chief asked Tony "Why is it that you come back to me and you leave this Simon Matembo in Africa?" My Chief was very angry at Tony. He yelled and shouted at Tony, HOW DARE HE COME HOME WITHOUT THIS SIMON MATEMBO!"

Winston's voice hit a new note and his audience shook with fear. Small children hid behind their parents as he stared hard at his audience.

"Tony, he tremble before the rage of my Chief. He told my chief that this boy would not come when he was asked. He told him that the people of Mapote say that his mother is a witch. He say that this boy will never leave his mother alone with people like these. When he hears this my Chief loses his anger. He say to Tony that it is not his fault. He say to Tony that this Simon Matembo must be a good boy because he will not leave his mother. He forgive Tony now. Then he speaks to me. He tells me to go and see those people of Mapote. He says I must bring feast for you. He says I must offer you great gifts."

Again a pause.

"Why does he offer these gifts? Because he wants this boy Simon Matembo to play football for him? What must you do for me to deliver these gifts? You must allow this boy's mother to come to Mapote and not call her a witch any more. This is what he has said. This woman is an educated woman. My Chief will pay for her to go to Kampala to learn to become a teacher. Whilst she is in Kampala he will build a fine school here in Mapote. This school will have a big football pitch. This school will have a satellite dish and a television to bring pictures from the sky. These pictures will show you this boy Simon Matembo and my boy Tony when they play for my Chief's football team.

"When the school is built this lady Rose Matembo will come back from Kampala and she will be the teacher for the children of Mapote. And the teacher will live in a fine hut in the village of Mapote. And the people of Mapote will show respect to the teacher.

"These are the words of my chief. These are the gifts of my chief. You must now decide these things."

Winston sat down on the stool and once again became a statue. Almost immediately a loud discussion broke out among the villagers of Mapote. The argument raged for over an hour and many longed for it to be finished so that they could start the feast. At last the Chief once again stood and waved for silence.

"We have listened to the message from The Great Chief of the Mersey. We have heard what he has said. We will do this thing that he asks. The boy Simon Matembo may go and play football for the Great Chief of the Mersey. The woman Rose Matembo will be our teacher and she will live amongst us with our respect. It is spoken."

Winston again rose and held out a hand to the chief. The chief winced at the hardness of Winston's grip. Winston said, "Tomorrow I will come with you to tell these things to Rose Matembo. Now we eat the feast."

The feast went on long into the night and the next morning there were many sore heads in the village of

Mapote. Tony, Samuel, Winston and the Chief made their way up the path to the hut at the top of the hill. The chief seemed rather worse for wear, but Winston was once again resplendent in his white robe.

It was hard to say what came as the greatest shock to Simon and Rose as they came out of their hut. Maybe it was the surprise at seeing Tony again. Maybe it was the even bigger surprise at seeing the chief of Mapote and his son at their door. Probably it was the sight of the giant man in the white robe. Tony stepped forward quickly and said. "Hello Rose, hello Simon" and he winked at them both.

Winston said. "Miss Rose Matembo. The Chief has things he would like to say to you. We will wait whilst he says these things."

The chief made his speech and Samuel translated for the benefit of Tony and Winston. The astonishment spread over the faces of Simon and his mother. At the end of his speech the chief bowed slightly. There was a silence. Tony looked to Simon. "I promised to do what I could. Will you come now?"

Simon was about to speak but his mother beat him to it. "He will go or I will never speak to him again."

As they talked Samuel guided Tony away from the group. As they looked down at the village below he said. "It is a wonderful thing that you have done Mr. Tony. Many of us younger people have felt bad about what has happened. I and my brother Thomas have felt bad for many years. It is the older men who have made up these stories. One day when I am chief I would have stopped this thing. I am glad that I do not now have to wait. Rose will be fine in Mapote now. The spell is broken. The spell was the foolishness of old men."

In the afternoon Tony and Winston collected Simon and

his mother and they drove over to see Father O'Malley. The news of the events of the evening before had already reached him and there was a twinkle in his eye as he led them into his small house.

"Well I've been hearing all manner of colourful stories this morning. I've heard of a giant in white sent to Mapote by the Great Chief of the Mersey. I gather that must be your good self Mr. Hobbes. Well, it's a pleasure to meet you." O'Malley noticed Winston's slightly embarrassed expression. "Now go away with you Mr. Hobbes. Don't be embarrassed with me. I always say that the Lord moves in mysterious ways. I don't care what you do so long as you've got the old men of Mapote to drop this ridiculous business."

O'Malley agreed to make all the arrangements to send Rose to Teacher Training college in Kampala. He also agreed to act as a banker and gave Tony details of his account in the capital. Tony said that he would send the money for the school and Rose's fees in instalments as and when they were requested by O'Malley. When all the arrangements were completed he smiled at Tony.

"It's a lot of money Tony. You're a generous man."

"Not at all. Once I get Simon here in the side I will pay all the bills out of my win bonuses."

"I'll believe you if you like," The old priest chuckled, "But I promise you that it isn't a sin for a footballer to have a heart."

The next morning Simon said a tearful goodbye to his mother and the three of them set off for Kampala. Once again when they were a few miles down the road Winston pulled up and changed. Simon looked on wide eyed as the big man climbed back into the cab wearing his jeans and a T-shirt. Winston clapped him on the back merrily.

"Don't look so worried boy. I had to put on a bit of an

act to get those old men to see a bit of sense. Underneath the fancy white robe I'm just an ordinary sort of guy."

"Ha!" snorted Tony. "Don't believe a word of it Simon. He's an absolute tyrant."

CHAPTER NINE

Back in the kingdom of the Mersey

It was a busy time for everyone as the three men arrived back in England at the beginning of February. Tony decided to be guided by Karen as to the pace they should set for Simon to settle in. For a week they simply drove him around and showed him the sights. It was almost too much for Simon to take in. Before coming to Liverpool, the biggest town that he had ever been to was the dusty little settlement at Kabale, and he had only ever been there three times.

He never seemed to lose a look of utter astonishment at everything that he saw. The only thing that did not enchant him was the weather, and even with three coats on he still shivered. Ben was delighted to see him again and after a few days he was well on the way to turning Simon into a fellow computer addict.

Tony made an appointment and went to see the Headmaster at the local secondary school. Initially the Head was most apologetic, but he said that it would be quite impossible for him to accept a pupil to do A' Levels if he had never sat any O' Levels. Tony pointed out that the boy had been very well educated, but it was still deemed impossible. Tony then pointed out that the boy was an exceptional footballer, and he could well help the school to success in the up-coming Northern Schools Championships and the Head felt that there just might be something that he could do. Tony then hinted that if the Head could find a place for Simon, he would personally be willing to come down after school on Thursdays to help coach the school team and the Head seemed quite sure that a place could be found.

Simon started school the following Monday. Karen smiled fondly as she watched him make his way inside looking tremendously smart in his new uniform. She had taken several pictures and mailed them to his mother. "Just imagine" she said, "first day at school and he's seventeen!"

"He's settling in well don't you think love?"

She squeezed his arm. "Oh he's fine Tony. The lad's had a hard tough life and it's standing him in good stead. I tell you, there won't be much that will bother young Simon. He's made from hard bark."

Simon did indeed settle well in his new school over the next fortnight and he was clearly delighted with his new life in England. Tony received more good news when he was given a clean bill of health to resume training. He played two reserve games and, although his touch was a bit out, he was well pleased with his general level of fitness. The leg held up fine and neither game was nearly as demanding as the Boxing Day battle in Misumba.

The first team were still having a bad time. They were rooted in mid-table and they had been bounced out of the League Cup by Sheffield Wednesday. The only hope left for the season was the FA Cup. So far the draw had treated them kindly. They had been given two home ties. The first round saw them cruise past non league Altrincham by 5–0. In the fourth round they had made horribly heavy weather of a seemingly straight forward tie against second division Millwall. A deflected goal in the last five minutes had saved them from an uncomfortable replay at the Den.

Round 5 saw them drawn away to Birmingham City who were riding high in Division 1. The tie was attracting great interest from the media who sensed an upset. The game was sold out weeks in advance. St. Andrews promised to be a hostile place to play.

Bill Jones watched Tony play his third reserve game and rather reluctantly selected him for the cup tie the following weekend. When Tony arrived home with three tickets for Winston and the two boys Simon was almost beside himself with excitement.

As the players underwent their preparations in the dressing room Tony was alarmed by the lack of confidence that filled the room. Jones was storming around getting more and more excited. "Now listen up. This is the FA Cup. We're away. It's a big crowd. They all hate us. I don't want anything fancy. We just sit back. We hit them hard. When we get the ball we bang it straight up for Vladimir. No poncy frills. Get the ball, bang it up. Simple."

Tony couldn't believe what he was hearing. Sure Birmingham were doing well, but they were a First

Division outfit when all was said and done. When were Liverpool ever this scared of a team from a lower division? It was crazy.

The first ten minutes were a nightmare. Birmingham flew at them like men possessed. The crowd bayed for blood. They hit the post and seemed to have a perfectly good goal disallowed. Liverpool hung on. Whenever they won the ball they simply hoofed it in the general direction of the big Bulgarian.

After twenty-five minutes play was held up due to a clash of heads. Tony waved several of the players over to him. They stood breathing deeply.

"OK, that's it. Jones may have forgotten what it means to play for Liverpool but I haven't. No more hoofing. From now on we get the ball and we keep it. Make them chase for it. They can't keep up this pace for ever. The next bloke who hoofs away possession will have me to deal with. Got it."They all nodded eagerly. When play resumed a vastly different Liverpool took shape. Tony started to pull all the strings. The noise from the stands eased and then went quiet.

Tony felt a confident energy surge through him. Every pass found its mark. Twice the Birmingham midfield tried to take him down and on both occasions he jinked out of the way with ease. He couldn't remember playing better.

As the crowd noise eased he could clearly hear the hysterical yelling of Bill Jones prowling the touchline. "Get it forward! Hit the long ball! Stop pussy footing about!"

Tony never even glanced at him. In the 43rd minute he collected the ball in the centre circle and sensed that there was space ahead of him. The pace of the game was obviously beginning to tell on his marker. He burst forward into the space. The centre half was drawn out to meet him and he slipped the ball just before he could make the tackle. He hurdled the sliding legs and ran on to meet the return pass. He looked up and saw Bobby Simms making a run to the back post. He clipped the ball over and Bobby gleefully headed it in.

They both ran to salute the rejoicing Liverpool Fans behind the goal and Tony spotted Simon leaping around with joy next to his father.

Five minutes later they were back into an altogether happier and more confident dressing room. Then Jones walked in. One of the younger players said. "What about that then boss! Classy or what?"

"Shut up you idiot!" Jones's voice was high pitched and shrill. He stormed over to Tony. "Now you listen Hobbo. I'm going to get something straight here. *I'm* the boss. *Not You! ME!* Now I gave instructions about tactics and you took it on yourself to change them. Now get your tracksuit on and get out of here, you're substituted."

There was an atmosphere of utter astonishment in the room. Tony could see no point in arguing, he simply pulled on his tracksuit and walked to the door. Before leaving he turned and said, "Keep it going boys. You've got them. Just keep at it . . . "

"I SAID GET OUT!!!"

He walked up the tunnel and was making his way to the bench when he spotted Sir Robert waving to him from the Director's Box. He climbed up the steps to where he waited.

"Don't tell me that your leg has flared up again Tony."

"No. The leg is fine."

The Chairman frowned. "So what on earth are you doing on the bench?"

"Jones substituted me."

"What! Why?"

"For interfering with his tactics. He told us to hit it long and kick them. I told the lads that we should play the Liverpool way. He didn't like it."

Sir Robert's face became a mask of anger. "Right. Thank you Tony."

The second half was almost unwatchable. Liverpool lost almost all of their rhythm and once again Birmingham hammered away at them. Somehow they held out, although the last five minutes felt more like five hours.

Tony was going round congratulating the shattered defenders when the dressing room door flew open. Sir Robert said. "Well done lads. Well fought. Come with me Mr. Jones. Now."

The players smirked at each other and wondered what was going on. Sir Robert returned alone five minutes later. He was still fuming mad. "This is not my usual style but it is hardly a usual situation. I have just given Mr. Jones an official warning. I have reminded him a little of the proud history of this football club. We will not allow our reputation to be dragged down. Tony, I apologise on behalf of the club for what has happened today and I promise that it will not happen again. Mr. Jones will consider his future over the weekend and if he decides to continue as our manager, it will be as the manager of a team playing football the Liverpool way. Thank you gentlemen, and once again, bloody well done."

Tony told the reporters that his leg had felt slightly weak and that they had thought it best not to risk the second half. Jones made his own way back to Liverpool. It meant that the rest of the team had a much happier coach ride back.

The next morning it was Tony's turn to be a spectator. Simon was making his debut for the school against Manchester Grammar School. Manchester had more or less ruled northern football for many years and they had not been beaten for well over a season. On the other hand Highfield, Simon's new school, had no great reputation on the football field. The games between the two schools were generally painfully one sided.

There was a stir of excitement among the watching parents when Tony took his place alongside the touchline with Ben. Several boys ran over to get his autograph and he was signing when he heard a voice behind him.

"Hello Hobbo." When he turned he was amazed to see that it was Jim McCaig. McCaig had been the hard man of the United midfield when Tony had first played at Old Trafford at the age of 19. Tony had ended that particular game bruised from head to toe and much wiser than when he had started. McCaig had come to the dressing room after the match to invite him for a drink. Later in the bar the tough little Scotsman had told Tony that he had done well and should go far. "I kicked you as hard as I know how and you still never went down and whinged. You're all right Tony," he had said in his Glasgow accent. Tony had always liked McCaig.

"Jimmy! Long time no see. What are you doing here? I thought your lad was all grown up now."

"He is." Said McCaig. "I'm working Tony. United have hired me as a scout. There's a couple of lads here that we're looking at. More to the point, what are you doing here? Has Jones got you scouting now?"

"No" laughed Tony, "I have a friend of the family who is playing his first game. Me and Ben thought we would give him a bit of support."

"Good on you. Mind if I stand with you?"

"Course not. In fact you can look after me if any of Brad Finnighan's mates find out that I'm in town."

79

McCaig glanced around to make sure nobody was listening. "Off the record Tony, that arrogant little devil deserved a good smacking. He's been a bit better for it since you took him down a peg."

Tony chuckled. As the game kicked off a thin rain started to fall. Manchester got the ball and started to pass it around with a confident ease. Highfield chased it half-heartedly. It was rather like watching a cat teasing a wounded mouse. Then Simon darted back from the centre circle and nicked the ball off one of the midfielders. He danced through four tackles and chipped the ball delicately into the top corner of the Manchester net. His new classmates mobbed him whilst the Manchester players looked at each other in amazement.

McCaig was transfixed. "I suppose that boy is the friend of the family Tony."

Tony grinned. "Sure is."

"And I suppose that he has an agent?"

"Sure has."

"And I suppose that his agent is your dad?"

"Right again."

"Mmmmm." McCaig never said another word as Simon went on to score eight goals in the first half. He didn't score any in the second half as he concentrated on setting up chances for his team mates. Highfield won 12–3.

McCaig turned to Tony as the boys left the pitch. "He's special Tony. I mean Georgie Best special."

"I know."

"Make sure that you look after him."

"Don't worry. I will."

Later that afternoon the balls were far from kind to Liverpool. They were drawn away to Newcastle in the FA Cup Quarter-Final.

CHAPTER TEN

New Recruit

After training the next day Tony drove back to Anfield to see Sir Robert. A rather sulky Bill Jones had taken training that morning, and he had made a point of spending most of the session practising short passing.

When Tony walked into his office Sir Robert asked "So how was it this morning Tony. Did I get the message across do you think?"

"No problem Sir Robert. I think you scared him half to death."

The Chairman nodded with satisfaction. "Good. I'm pleased. Now what can I do for you?"

"Are you busy tomorrow morning?"

Sir Robert scanned his diary. "Not bad. Why?"

"Come down to training at nine o'clock. I'm bringing a lad down to have a run out with the lads. I'd like you to see him."

Sir Robert sat back in his chair and gave a small smile.

"This all sound rather interesting. Is he good?"

Tony smiled back. "Make your own mind up."

The next morning was bright and sunny. Tony had agreed with the Headmaster that Simon could have the morning off school. There were looks of surprise and amusement as Tony and Simon walked over to where the players were gathered.

Jones rolled his eyes. "So what's this Hobbo? We're not running a nursery here you know."

"I know that boss." Said Tony. He pointed to where Sir Robert was climbing out of his Jag on the car park. "The Chairman wants to have a look at this lad. Could you just set up a quick twenty minute game?"

The sight of Sir Robert striding over the grass soon had an effect on Jones. "Yeah, sure, no problem."

Tony grinned at the confused expressions of his fellow players. "Morning lads. Meet a pal of mine. This is Simon Matembo. Be nice to him won't you."

To start with the players took Tony literally. They thought that Simon must have been the son of some important client and they took care to give him space. When he scored his second goal they got the message. This was no rich kid being given the red carpet treatment by the club. This was a serious trial.

For twenty minutes they tried all they could to tackle him. Some of the time they managed it. Other times they didn't. Simon scored two more goals and showed the full range of his breathtaking skills. When Jones blew his whistle they all looked on with complete astonishment.

Simon trotted over to Tony who said. "Good effort lad." Then to his team mates. "Thanks boys. I'll be with you in a minute."

Simon grinned from ear to ear. "Thank you all for the

game. I enjoyed it very much."

They went over to Sir Robert. "Simon, this is Sir Robert Hyde, the Chairman of the club. I suppose you would call him the Chief."

Sir Robert shook the boy's hand and said. "I'm delighted to meet you Simon."

In a formal voice Simon replied. "For me it is indeed the very greatest honour sir."

The Chairman glanced quickly to Tony. "A strange accent, where are you from Simon?"

"I am from Mapote. It is in Uganda. But I have a passport for the United Kingdom. I live with Mr. Tony now."

The boy's manners made Sir Robert smile. "How do you like England Simon?"

"It is wonderful. I am very happy. Liverpool is my new home. And Liverpool are my team. I see them in the cup match at Birmingham. One day I would like to play in this team with Mr. Tony."

"Oh, and one day you will Simon. You may be sure of that." Tony said. "You'd best go and get changed now Simon. Come out and watch the training when you're ready."

They watched as the young African loped over to the pavilion to change.

Sir Robert spoke in a wistful voice. "When I was 13 years old my Granddad took me to Anfield to watch Liverpool play United. It was 1963. I saw a young lad called George Best play. I haven't seen anyone like him for thirty years. Until this morning. Should I talk terms with Winston?"

"Yes. But not all of them. Some you talk about with me."

"Go on."

"I won't see him rushed. He's only seventeen and England is a heck of a shock to the system after Mapote. I've got him into school and he's doing his A' Levels. That

is what is most important for the next two years. No
Media. No hype. I would like him to come down and
work with Walter Simpson and the reserves. Maybe he
could play a game or two for the reserves, but school has
to come first.

"I've never seen anything like him Sir Robert, but I made
a promise to his mother to look after him. Let's take it easy.
Remember what happened to Georgie Best?"

Sir Robert nodded. "Wise words Tony. You are your
father's son. Liverpool Football Club will do things any
way you like, just so long as Simon signs on the dotted line."

Tony was delighted. "That's fantastic. Talk to Dad about
money and me about football. He can take us back to the
great days you know."

The Chairman grinned wolfishly. "Oh, I know that all
right. Look out Manchester, the Liverpool Leopard is
waiting in the woods."

"Liverpool Leopard?"

"Why not?"

Tony thought for a moment. "Yeah. Why not."

Much happened over the following three weeks. Winston
and Sir Robert fought it out for hour after hour until a
contract was at last signed. It was a ten year contact with a
host of bonuses and incentives built in that would make it
possible for Simon Matembo to become one of the richest
footballers on the planet.

Tony played in the next three league games and
Liverpool strung together two wins and a draw to move
up to seventh in the table. Simon was allowed to miss
school on Tuesday and Thursday mornings to train with
the reserves and he made his debut as a substitute on a wet
March night away at Derby. When he came on with ten
minutes to go the team was trailing by one goal to nil. Six

minutes later Simon had scored twice. His second goal was an amazing jinking run from the half way line. He beat five defenders and rocketed in a shot.

The goal was watched by a crowd numbering 1,243. None of them would ever forget seeing Simon Matembo make his debut in a Liverpool shirt. The following Saturday Tony led the side out to meet Newcastle in the quarter final. It soon turned into a classic match. Both teams were well matched as the ball fizzed around the pitch in quick passing moves. The Geordies took the lead in the 29th minute but Liverpool were back on level terms before half time. Tony revelled in the speed of the game and found once again that his passing was at its best.

The second half was a feast of open attacking football. Both goalkeepers performed heroically on many occasions. Liverpool at last scored their winning goal in the 78th minute.

As the players celebrated in the dressing room they heard the news of the semi-final draw. It was Arsenal. Arsenal at Villa Park. They had avoided United. United had drawn the easiest tie and were to play Ipswich at Hillsborough.

Tony sat drinking a can of lager and thought that one more win would bring on his rematch with Brad Finnighan. A rematch at Wembley! He felt fit and in the form of his life. It couldn't come quickly enough.

But first they would have to deal with Arsenal.

They won their next two games and the press were beginning to write in glowing terms about the new flowing style. The semi-final confrontation was shaping up to be a real battle. Arsenal were a hard, no nonsense side who had been grinding out results all season. They had hung on grimly to United in the league and were still only a point behind. They were rugged and tough. Nobody conceded less goals.

Meanwhile Simon played two more games in the reserves. In the first he again came on as a substitute and scored. In the second he played the full game and scored a hat trick in front of a gleeful crowd at Anfield. The crowd was in fact much larger than was normal for a reserve game. Word was leaking out about the new boy from Africa with the magical skills. The Leopard. More and more local reporters were turning up at Tony's door begging for interviews with the Leopard. They were all turned away.

On the Wednesday before the semi final the disaster started. Two players had to finish training early due to feeling unwell. The next day three more players were unable to train. By Friday seven first team squad members were in bed with a heavy dose of flu.

Bill Jones was tearing his hair out. The club was going to have to take the field at Villa Park the following Sunday with a severely weakened team.

Jones caught up with Tony as he was walking back to the pavilion after training. "Got a minute Hobbo?"

"Sure."

"Could you pop over to Anfield. Sir Robert would like a word."

"Of course," said Tony thoughtfully. What could it be?

Sir Robert seemed slightly uneasy when Tony walked into his office. Tony sat whilst the Chairman stood and looked out of the window onto the pitch. Eventually he turned and spoke.

"We're in trouble Tony. This flu has really wrecked the team. Please tell me that you are OK."

"I'm fine boss."

"Thank goodness. Now listen. I know that a deal is a deal, and I would never back out of a deal. But we need help Tony. I can't see a way to beat Arsenal on Sunday, not with all the injuries. Jones has been to see me. He wants to put Simon in the squad. I know that it is a desperate move, but I'm afraid that we are desperate. I told him about how Simon's contract works for the next two years, and strangely enough he agreed fully that it was a good idea. However, I promised him that I would talk to you. Well, I'm talking. This is a huge game for the club. We need him Tony."

Tony sat quietly. It was a big decision. He had carefully mapped things out for Simon and he was determined to shelter the boy from the limelight for as long as he could. But was that fair? Tony had been given his Liverpool debut as a teenager so why not Simon. He remembered Karen's words and he could only agree that the boy was indeed very tough. The Chairman was right. The game at Villa Park was the most important game that the club had faced for several years. He came to his decision.

"OK Sir Robert, I agree, but only on my terms. He will sit on the sub's bench. It will be my decision as to whether or not he comes on. If we are winning he stays on the bench. If we are getting hammered and it is a lost cause he stays on the bench. If I feel that he will make the difference, then I will signal for him to come on. OK?"

The Chairman was relieved. "Yes, that is more than fair. Thanks Tony."

Tony gave Simon the news when he collected him from school later that afternoon. The boy's face glowed with excitement.

THE DRUMS OF ANFIELD

CHAPTER ELEVEN

Villa Park

 It was like walking out into a sea of noise as Tony led the team out onto the Villa Park pitch the following Sunday. The club had managed to keep the story of the flu bug under wraps and therefore the fans were astonished to see such an unusual looking Liverpool side take the field. Four young players were making their first team debuts. Tony sensed a buzz of anticipation amongst the Liverpool fans as they watched Simon warm up in his tracksuit.

In the first half things went better than he could have hoped. The new players were well coached. They slotted in nicely to the Liverpool passing style and as a result the team enjoyed long periods of possession. Arsenal's way was to sit back and soak up pressure, and the fact that Liverpool were fielding such a weakened side made no difference to the Londoners' style of play.

When the referee blew for half time Tony was pretty happy with the performance. His only concern was that Liverpool had failed to create a single clear cut chance.

Every effort had been brushed aside by the mighty Arsenal defence.

Things soon changed in the second half. The Arsenal manager had really got his team fired up. They started to hammer away at Liverpool and the pressure grew steadily. In the 68th minute they finally broke through as their centre half headed home from a corner.

Tony tried to lift the players but it was difficult. The younger players were tiring and the Arsenal defenders were finding it easier and easier to break down the Liverpool attacks.

Play was halted whilst a player received treatment. Tony glanced over to the touchline where Simon was energetically running up and down. Bill Jones was standing out of the dugout and giving him a pleading look.

It was time. They needed Simon. Tony nodded to Jones and he quickly waved Simon over to tell him to get ready. He came on three minutes later to wild cheers from the Liverpool end.

There were still fifteen minutes of the game left.

Tony managed to slip the ball to him a couple of minutes later. The stadium held its breath as he slipped past the two central defenders and chipped the keeper. The ball seemed to hang in the air for an eternity before dropping onto the cross bar. The Arsenal keeper dived on the ball gratefully.

Simon's break scared the Londoners to death. Their frantic manager shouted instructions and immediately two men moved over to mark Simon. Arsenal did all they could to waste time and keep possession. Tony felt a rising panic as Liverpool chased and chased to try and get the ball.

The clock was ticking down. Six minutes to go. At last he made a big tackle in the centre of the field. He sensed Simon spin and break fast down the right wing. He flipped the ball forward and cursed himself. It was too high.

As he ran forward he saw Simon jump high with his back arched. Somehow he seemed to twist in the air and take the ball on his chest. As he was dropping he clipped the ball over the last defender. He hit the ground and he was away.

Tony drove himself forward with every ounce of energy that he had left in his body. The last defender pounded across and slid into a tackle on the African. He had no intention of winning the ball. He was looking to deposit Simon in the second row of the stand. Simon managed to jump the instant before the tackle hit him full-on. Still the defender caught his leg and he landed awkwardly.

For a moment it seemed that he couldn't possibly keep his footing. For three strides it looked a certainty that he would fall. Then, at last, he regained his balance and caught the ball just before it crossed the goal line.

Tony was arriving in the penalty area at full speed. Simon whipped a cross over. It was too far. Too far. Tony didn't think that he could make it. His lungs were on fire. He threw himself into a dive. He stretched his neck. He stretched every part of his body and the ball hit his forehead with a meaty thump. A split second before he hit the ground he saw the ball flying toward the top corner like a bullet.

As he crashed to the ground the stadium seemed to explode. The massed ranks of the Liverpool fans were behind the goal where Tony had scored. They went absolutely berserk. As he picked himself up off the floor he saw Simon jogging back from the touchline giving the supporters a shy wave. Then they were both mobbed by their team mates.

Tony had to shake them off and shout. "Right. That's

enough. Pack it in. We're not there yet. We *don't* want extra time. Come on. Concentrate. Get tight."

As he watched them restart the game Tony could see that the Arsenal team had been hit hard by the goal. They were vulnerable. If the game went into extra time they would soon regain their composure and realise just how tired the inexperienced Liverpool players were. For five minutes the game was bogged down in the centre of the park as both sets of players flew at each other.

Tony received a short pass and was looking for Simon when he found himself in mid-air. The Arsenal centre forward had crashed into him from behind. As he hit the ground in a heap he heard the whistle blow and the Liverpool end of the ground resounded with boos. There could only be seconds to go.

He grabbed the ball and heaved himself quickly to his feet. Simon was ten yards away. He gave him the ball. The Arsenal team were surprised by the speed of the free kick.

Simon turned as he took the ball. He started to run for goal. Tony's chest was pounding and his legs felt like lead weights. The foul had taken all the wind from him. He could do no more than stand and watch.

The scene that unfolded was absolutely breathtaking. Simon glided past four wild tackles and rounded the keeper before rolling the ball slowly into the net.

Within seconds his slim frame was completely submerged by the red shirts of his team mates. He heard the referee blow his whistle three times. Full time. It was over. They had done it.

Tony sank down to the ground and fought to catch his breath. The ground rocked with the noise of the Liverpool supporters. The other players had lifted Simon to their shoulders and they were taking the acclaim of the fans.

John Higgins, the Arsenal centre-half and captain, walked slowly over to where Tony was sitting and held out a hand. Tony took it and the Arsenal player heaved him to his feet. They had played in the England team years before and had shared a room for away games.

"Great game Hobbo."

"Thanks John. You too." He was still so short of breath that he could hardly speak.

Higgins shook his head as both men watched the players bounce Simon up and down on their shoulders.

"I've never seen anything like him Hobbo. Never."

"Neither have I. He's special."

"Well I hope he does the same to United Hobbo."

Tony grinned. "Me too."

When he was at last put down onto the floor Simon trotted over to where Tony still waited on the half way line. "Are you OK Mr. Tony?"

Tony had to laugh when he saw the look of serious concern on Simon's face. "Of course I am. Just a bit winded, that's all. Otherwise I've never felt better in my life. Come on, let's get you back to the dressing room. No reporters, OK?"

"OK Mr. Tony. It was a very great header."

"It was a very great cross."

They both laughed as they left the pitch. The dressing room was a place of celebration. News came in from Hillsborough that United had cruised past Ipswich 3–0. So the dream final was to be after all.

The dressing-room was soon under siege from reporters demanding to interview Simon. Tony took a long swig of water and went out to handle them. The first interview was with Andy Gray of *Sky TV* who had screened the match live.

He talked to Tony as they set up the microphone.

"Come on Hobbo. Surely you'll give us a quick word with the new lad."

"No Andy. No interviews. Not yet. Give the lad a break. He's only a kid."

Gray was desperate. "Give me a break will you! The whole world'll want to hear him after what he just did. I've never seen anything like it! Please Hobbo, name your price."

Tony chuckled. "Calm down Andy. The world is just going to have to be patient and so are you. The answer is no and there is no price. You'll just have to make do with me."

A deep, loud voice spoke from behind them. It was Winston. "Is this television man givin' you trouble Tony?"

Gray groaned. "Hello Winston."

"Hello Andy. This boy is not ready for any TV yet. When he is ready I will tell you. Now you talk to Tony."

Tony worked his way through several interviews and it was forty minutes before he was able to get back to the dressing room to shower and change. When they left the ground to get on the coach there were hundreds of Liverpool fans waiting to cheer them.

Tony sat alone at the front of the coach as it made its way back up the M6 to Liverpool. He enjoyed the quiet and the sense of triumph. He was delighted when he glanced back up the bus to see Simon laughing and joking with a group of the younger players. What a day! Five young players had pulled on first team shirts for the first time and they had broken through the mighty Arsenal defence and made it to Wembley. One player had done more than that. Simon Matembo had shown the world that a huge new talent was born.

His life would never be the same again.

CHAPTER TWELVE

Disaster Strikes

Tony awoke the next morning in a fantastic mood. The April sun was shining strongly through the bedroom window and all seemed well with his world. He pulled on his dressing gown and looked out. A knot of reporters were camped out on the pavement outside the house. It wasn't much of a surprise. they could wait there all week as far as he was concerned.

He went downstairs and switched on the kettle. He pulled a £10 note from his wallet and went into the lounge where Ben and Simon were watching the television.

"Morning lads. Lovely morning. Ben, take this tenner and pop down to the newsagent and buy a copy of every paper that you can find. I'm afraid that you better not go with him Simon, there's a gang of reporters outside . . . "

His voice trailed off as he noticed their faces. Ben looked pale and worried. Tears were running down Simon's cheeks. Tony was aghast. "Good Lord. What on earth has happened."

Ben pointed to the TV screen. "Look Dad. It's terrible. There's been a volcano in Uganda. It is near Mapote."

Simon spoke very softly. "It is a mountain in the Ruwenzori. We call it Batumba, *The Evil One*. It is many years since it has exploded. Old men tell of how things are when Batumba is angry. When Batumba is angry things are very bad in Mapote."

Tony sat down slowly and watched the pictures on the screen with horror. A huge pillar of smoke and dust had climbed high into the sky from the volcano. The reporter was speaking into his microphone under the shelter of a veranda. He explained that millions of tonnes of volcanic dust were falling across a huge area of eastern Uganda. As well as the dust there had been rocks thrown from the volcano like artillery shells. Some of these rocks were the size of cars and many casualties were reported.

The whole area had been plunged into chaos and the emergency services were quite unable to cope. The hospital at Kabale was already full to overflowing.

The report finished with several shots which showed how the beautiful rolling green hills were now coated in a choking layer of volcanic ash.

Simon spoke in a small voice. "Mr. Tony. I must go back. I must find out if my mother is OK. I cannot stay here."

Tony nodded. "Of course you must. But let me think."

He made his coffee and forced himself to think clearly. He remembered the small, pot holed roads that led from Kampala to Mapote. It was a two day drive even in the best of times. How long would it take now? By the time that they got a flight and found a car . . . it would take at least a week. He stopped himself as he realised that he was thinking in terms of *we*. Well of course he was. There was no way that he would allow Simon to return alone, no way at all.

He considered the complications and remembered with relief that there was no football for a fortnight. The following weekend had been left clear to allow for preparations for the next England international. Even so, the club would not be happy about him going off to the disaster area in Uganda. He brushed the thought aside. The club would have to lump it.

He racked his brain. There was no way that he could allow Simon to have to wait a whole week for news of his mother. The tension would be awful for the boy. But what else could he do. There were very few phones in the Mapote district and he felt that those which were there were would almost certainly be damaged. Then an idea hit him.

He grabbed the phone and started to make calls. It took him five calls before he had the information that he needed – Andy Gray's home number.

He dialled and drummed his fingers impatiently as he waited for an answer. Gray's unmistakable Scottish voice came on the line. "Hello."

"Andy. It's Tony Hobbes speaking."

Surprised. "Oh, morning Hobbo, what can I do for you?"

"Yesterday you asked me to name a price for you to get an interview with Simon. I have a price."

"Go on."

"Have you seen the news?"

Gray sounded confused. "Well yes and no. I've had the radio on. I haven't really listened though."

"Have you heard about the volcano in Uganda."

"Yes, I heard something."

Tony took a deep breath. "Good. Now listen. Simon comes from a village that is right in the middle of the disaster area. His mother is there and the poor lad is worried sick. He wants to go straight back but there is no way that we will be able to get there for days. Now *Sky* have a news team in the area. I've just watched their report. If you can get them to go to Mapote and find out about his mum, we will give you an exclusive interview."

Gray sounded concerned. "This is awful Hobbo. Don't worry. I'll do what I can. Wait by the phone."

"One more thing Andy. Please don't give the story any publicity until you find out how the news is. I don't want Simon to get any bad news from the television. If the news is good and Rose is OK you will have a great story and an exclusive interview."

"Leave it with me Hobbo. Tony went back into the lounge and told Simon what was happening. Gray called back half an hour later and told him that *Sky* were contacting their team in Uganda and sending them to Mapote.

The day seemed to last for ever as they sat and waited for the phone to ring. By four in the afternoon Tony's nerves were stretched to breaking point when the phone started to ring. He gabbed the receiver. "Hobbo, it's Andy here. It's good news. Our people made it through to the village and they found out that Rose Matembo is in her college in Kampala. The village is not too badly damaged. There weren't too many hits by the big rocks it seems. There are one or two injuries but nothing serious. The bad news is the coffee crop. It's destroyed. There will be no harvest this year."

Tony sagged with relief and immediately told Simon the wonderful news. He resumed his conversation. "I can't thank you enough for this Andy. I owe you one."

The Scot chuckled. "And you'll pay me one too."

All through the afternoon news coverage of the disaster the television had been advertising the number for a relief fund which had been set up to provide much needed aid to the stricken region. As Tony sat down the number was once again on the screen. Simon said. "Mr. Tony. Is there anything that we could do to help this fund? With no coffee there will be a very bad time in Mapote."

Tony sat back and thought. As he thought his gaze fell upon a picture on the wall. As he stared at the picture the germ of an idea grew in his mind. The more he stared, the more it grew. At last he leapt to his feet and clapped his hands. "Yes Simon. There is something. It is a real long shot, but I think there is definitely something that we can do."

He made several more calls and then left the house. He completely ignored the gaggle of reporters and jumped into his car. He drove to a hotel on the outskirts of the city and one by one the other players arrived. When they were all gathered he stood up and spoke to them.

"OK guys, listen up. You probably don't know, but that big volcano that has gone off in Uganda is right by the place where Simon lives. Now there is a big appeal for help and I for one am going to do something. I have something in mind. If it comes off it will mean all of us going to Uganda. Now let me tell you all about it . . . "

An hour later he left the hotel. All the players were with him. His next stop was the Chairman's house. They talked for two hours but in the end Sir Robert agreed to allow them to go. "If you can pull it off in Cape Town and get *Sky* on board you can leave all the detailed arrangements to the club. The last thing you will want to be worrying about is visas and hotel bookings. Best of luck Tony. You deserve it."

His last call was his father's house. He had kept his dad informed of events in Uganda all day but he hadn't told him of his plan. As he walked into the house he said to Winston. "Right dad. Upstairs and pack a bag. We need to be on the road in half an hour. I have a hotel room booked at Heathrow and if we move now we'll make it before midnight. You'll need two days off work."

Winston raised his hands to slow Tony down. "Now steady on boy and talk to me properly. What do I need a bag for? Why are we goin' to Heathrow? Where are we goin'?"

"South Africa. I've booked the tickets and we land in Cape Town tomorrow evening."

When Tony explained why, his father was more than happy to take two days off work.

CHAPTER THIRTEEN

Pay for View

Tony, Winston and Simon took the 5 a.m. flight from Heathrow and landed in Cape Town many hours later. They were all exhausted by the flight and they went quickly off to bed in their hotel after a quick snack. Before he turned off the lights Tony placed a call to England and spoke again to Andy Gray.

"Did you find anything out Andy?"

"Yes. You're a lucky boy Hobbo. He will be at the Residence all morning and according to his official diary there doesn't seem to be anything planned."

"Brilliant." Tony was hugely relieved. "What are the people at *Sky* saying?"

"If you can come up with the goods tomorrow they are happy to back you."

More good news. "Listen, that's fantastic Andy. Thanks for all your help."

"Don't mention it. You still owe me that interview remember."

Tony laughed. "Well I don't think you are likely to let me forget it in a hurry."

They ate breakfast early and climbed into a taxi a little after eight. The sleep had put Winston in a growly mood and he grumped and groaned for the whole journey. "This is the most stupid thing I have ever done. This man is one of the busiest men in the world. He's not goin' to find time to see two bit people like us. You just wait and see. This is just a wild goose chase . . . "

At last the taxi dropped them off outside a huge set of metal gates which were guarded by a police post. Two policemen stepped out to meet them as they approached the gates.

"Can we help you gentlemen?"

"Yes." Said Tony brightly. "We would like to see President Mandela."

The policeman first looked quite bemused, then a small recognition came into his eyes. "You are Tony Hobbes. Liverpool captain, yes?"

Tony beamed. "That is correct."

"Do you have an appointment?"

"No."

"Then what you ask is quite impossible Mr. Hobbes."

Tony reached into his shoulder-bag and pulled out the picture from his lounge wall which had caught his attention the afternoon before. It was a picture of himself and President Nelson Mandela, and it had been taken nine years before when Liverpool had toured South Africa. The photo had been taken after a game that the club had played in the township of Soweto. The club had been reluctant to play the game due to violence in the surrounding area. Tony had persuaded the players to go ahead with the game and President Mandela had been very grateful.

"Please take this to him and tell him that I am waiting outside. I need to discuss a very urgent matter. It will only take a few minutes."

The policemen looked doubtful but he went into the command post and spoke on the telephone. A few minutes later a man in a suit came to collect the photo. A further twenty minutes passed before the man in the suit returned. He spoke quickly to the policemen and then came over to Tony.

"Mr. Hobbes. Our President sends his compliments. He will see you now."

Tony turned to wink at his father as they were led along a succession of long corridors. Simon was like a mouse. As they were ushered into a fine old office Nelson Mandela rose from the desk and smiled. He was older than when Tony had last seen him but he still had a remarkable presence.

"Well Tony. What a pleasant surprise. I apologise that you were kept waiting. Please introduce me to your colleagues. In fact, wait a minute. I already know this boy. If I am not mistaken you are Simon Matembo. I think all of South Africa saw your goal at the weekend. Please sit down."

Coffee was brought and Mandela asked politely about their flight and hotel. He never mentioned the unorthodox nature of their arrival. "Now Tony, you said that you came with urgent business?"

"Indeed Mr. President. You will be aware of the situation in Uganda?"

Mandela frowned. "Indeed I am. The situation is grave."

Tony pressed on. "Well Simon comes from a village in the centre of the disaster area. A place called Mapote. He asked me if there was anything that we can do to help the relief appeal. Well I think that there is, but I will need your help."

Mandela was intrigued. "Continue please."

"Well." Said Tony, "I have had discussions with my fellow players and the management of the club. I have also had discussions with *Sky TV*. In a nutshell, our team is willing to go to Uganda to play a game to raise money for the Appeal. *Sky* are willing to show the game on *Pay for View* all over the world and donate the proceeds to the relief appeal. We have three very famous pop groups who will come out with us and perform live before the game. Everything is nearly in place. All we need now is some opposition. I think that we should play South Africa. Now that is where I need your help."

Mandela laughed aloud with delight at the idea. "Tony, is this really all your own idea?"

"Amazingly enough, yes, it is."

"Then you are to be congratulated. Of course we will field a side, hopefully a good side. Tell me, have you made arrangements yet with the Ugandan Government?"

"No. I waited to speak with you before talking to them."

"No problem. Please leave all of that to me. I know President Kumba well. We are old friends. All you need to do is turn up and all will be arranged. When is the game to be?"

"I'm afraid that the only time that Liverpool and *Sky* can fit it in is next Sunday."

Mandela whistled. "Five days. Not very long, but long enough. We shall have to be quick on our feet. The good news is that I have a free weekend and so I shall be able to come myself. I look forward to seeing more of you young man."

He smiled at Simon who was acutely embarrassed. "Thank you sir." was all that he could manage to say.

The next few days seemed to pass in a blur. Within hours of their meeting with the President, *Sky* started to put their advertising machine into overdrive. They sent a news team to Kampala to meet Tony, Winston and Simon when they got off the plane from Cape Town. There were huge crowds of Ugandans at the airport to cheer their new hero. The promised interview was carried out in the garden of their hotel, and the camera crew then filmed them as they travelled around. They visited the stadium that would hold the match on the following Sunday. They visited Rose at her college and took tea with President Kumba in his palace where he gave Simon a humorous ticking-off for adopting a British passport. Finally they were flown by helicopter to Mapote where the chief took them on a tour of the damaged areas.

Tony was appalled at the devastation. The choking grey ash seemed to have coated everywhere and everything. However the prospect of the match had lifted everyone's spirits. Tony had arranged for the government to lay on buses so that the whole of Mapote could go to Kampala to watch their newly adopted son. Despite the thick coat of ashes, it was still possible to see that building work on the new school was well under way.

The team arrived in Kampala on Saturday afternoon and they shared a hotel with the South African squad. Tony had a drink with their captain that evening and they agreed that the game should be competitive without being silly. Neither side wanted injuries.

The excitement in Kampala the next day was enormous. The small stadium couldn't begin to hold the many thousands who yearned to see the game. Andy Gray arrived on the same plane as Karen and Tony's mum that morning. They all told Tony that the interest in the UK was unbelievable. Everyone wanted to see more of Simon. Andy said that *Sky* had been staggered by the number of advance bookings they had taken.

It was well into the African night when the two teams took to the field. The crowd was a blaze of noise and colour. The mesmeric beat of hundreds of drums made the warm air seem to bounce. The pop groups had all performed and the stage was set. Presidents Kumba and Mandela were introduced to the two teams and at last the match kicked off.

The South Africans were fast and skilful and they adapted to the hard bumpy pitch much better than Liverpool. The Englishmen soon realised that they were up against it and their professional pride made them play hard. The game was played at an unrelenting speed. At half time South Africa led by 2–1. The second half saw two moments of utter brilliance from Simon and the game eventually ended 3–3.

A jubilant Andy Gray came into the dressing room soon after the final whistle where both sets of players were sharing a beer. He told them that *Sky* had sold in excess of two million pay for view packages. They had raised more than £20,000,000 for the relief fund.

Winston came over to Tony as all the players cheered at the news. He shook his son's hand. "Tony, I have never been so proud. No man has ever been so proud. You have done a very great thing here."

Another visitor came into the dressing room and the noise immediately died down. President Nelson Mandela was wearing the very widest of smiles. He came over to Tony and Winston.

"Now," he said. "You asked me for a favour and I was happy to help. Now it is my turn to ask for a favour. I know everybody must ask you the same thing but I demand to be placed at the head of the queue. I am visiting Europe next month and I would like you to get me a ticket for the Cup Final."

Tony grinned. "Oh, I think I might just be able to work something out."

CHAPTER FOURTEEN

Twin Towers

It took several days for everyone to get over the Ugandan trip. Leicester City contacted the club and volunteered to put their next match off for a fortnight which was a huge help. Football was riding high on the staggering level of funds raised by the game in Kampala.

As April drifted into May and the season wound to a close there were many very unhappy people in the media. The Simon Matembo story had become the biggest in the football world. Journalists from all over the world flocked to Anfield for the next Liverpool home game against Coventry. They were to be bitterly disappointed. Simon wasn't even on the bench. He made no appearance in the next game either. Speculation started to become almost frenzied.

Simon was in fact still training two mornings a week and he made three full appearances for the reserves. These games drew record crowds. By the third week in April the hype was getting out-of-hand and Tony and Sir Robert held a press conference to explain the nature of Simon's contract with Liverpool. The world was informed that for the next year school was to come first.

The conference did some good. However there was still one question that was being asked in pubs and schools and workshops all over the country. What about the Cup Final? Would he play in the Cup Final?

The nearer the big day came, the more the game was discussed. Journalists soon started to say that it was the most eagerly anticipated Cup Final that there had ever been. It did indeed have all the classic ingredients. United had finished the season strongly and had duly collected their third title in four years. Liverpool also had a strong finish.

The team was now well-established in its new style. They won five out of their last seven games and climbed to fourth in the table. It was to be a clash between the country's two form teams. To add spice to the occasion it was also a clash between two of the fiercest rivals in world football. To add even more spice it was to be the first meeting of Tony and Brad Finnighan since the incident at Old Trafford at the start of the season.

There was no doubting the mood of the nation. United had been becoming increasingly unpopular over the years. People resented their vast wealth and success. Liverpool on the other hand were riding on the crest of a wave. Their fund raising game against the South Africans had won them a place in the hearts of almost every neutral.

Most pundits agreed that United were probably the stronger side. Their team was battle hardened and littered with internationals from all over the world. They would be playing for the Double. Various interviews showed that their players held a huge resentment at the wave of public support for their arch rivals from the Mersey.

Two individual battles intrigued everyone. First there was Tony against Brad Finnighan. Finnighan had been voted *Player of the Year* by both the press and his fellow professionals. He had played quite magnificently for the whole season. He had become the hub of the United midfield. It was generally agreed that to stop United, you had to stop Finnighan. Could Tony Hobbes do this? At 33, would he have the fitness and the stamina to hunt the Irishman down over the open spaces of Wembley? Most of the experts believed that he could not. He was too old. His day had passed.

Even more intriguing was the prospect of Simon Matembo being subjected to man to man marking by United's Claudio Torrini. Torrini had been brought in from Inter Milan at the start of the season. He was an experienced Italian international and he specialising in snuffing players out of any game. At times his play was far from pretty to watch. He had collected 11 yellow cards through the season and he had become the man that all opposition fans loved to hate. If Matembo DID play there was little doubt who would be given the job of taking him out.

All the media hype soon got to Simon. A week after they returned from Kampala he approached Tony. "Mr. Tony, I know that school is the most important thing. My mother says the same thing. But I would like to play in the Cup Final. Just this one game. Even as a substitute."

Tony smiled at the boy. "Don't worry Simon. You'll be there at Wembley. I am not at all sure that we can beat United without you. But listen, you must not say a word about it to anyone, not even Ben. We are going to keep them guessing. Every day that goes by will make them more nervous. They won't really know how to prepare. That is how we want it. OK?"

Simon smiled with relief. "Yes. This is OK?"

"Now" Said Tony. "In the meantime you are going to help me. Come into the lounge and sit down. We are going to watch lots of videos of Brad Finnighan. He is good, really good, probably the best attacking midfielder that we have seen in ten years. He is clever with the ball and he is fast. He has a lot of tricks up his sleeve and he will use every one of them at Wembley. I want you to watch these tricks and learn them. There is nothing that he can do that you can't. When you have learned them we will go down to the training ground early in the mornings and you will try them out on me. OK?"

"Of course Mr. Tony."

Throughout the last two weeks in April and the first week in May they went to the training pitch a little after six in the morning. Time and time again Simon ran at Tony with the ball. To start with he flew by him two times out of three. By the second week Tony was able to make the tackle about half the time. By the end of the third week he got the ball three times out of four.

In the afternoons Tony cycled and swam. He went for mile after mile and length after length. By the week before the Final he was fitter than he had ever been before.

During the last week Simon joined the first team for training. They practised far away from the road so that nobody could watch. They worked hard on a variety of moves. Tony imitated Torrini and he dogged Simon around the pitch.

Still the club said nothing about the team. When the players moved to their hotel in Essex on the Friday morning Simon went to school as usual. He drove down with the family later in the evening. They entered the hotel by the back door.

The next morning the nation watched the shots of the team getting onto the coach for the drive to Wembley. No Simon Matembo. There was almost a sense of misery in the television studio. Simon in fact had arrived at Wembley with Winston before the coach had even left the hotel.

That morning there was a new sound to be heard from Liverpool to North London. It was heard in service station car parks and on railway platforms. It was heard in the pubs around Wembley. It was heard in the streets that lead to the famous old stadium. And as the time for kick off approached it was heard louder and louder.

It was the sound of drums.

An enterprising company in Southport had made the inspired move of importing thousands and thousands of small drums from a company in South Africa.

As the Liverpool fans converged on Wembley it seemed that almost every one of them carried a drum. At first the stewards wondered whether they should be allowed into the stadium. They consulted with the policeman in charge. He decided that it would be against the new mood of the game to confiscate the drums. They were allowed in.

As the players got ready in the dressing room they began to hear the sound. It was an awesome sound. There were nearly 20,000 drums in the stadium and when they were beaten together, it seemed to make the ground shake.

At the other end of the ground the United fans were reduced to near silence every time the sound of the drums beat across the stadium. To go with the sound of the drums was the chant of *"Matembo! Matembo! MATEMBO!"* The United supporters had been convinced that Simon would not play. At 2.30 their hopes were shattered. The drums thumped hard when the tannoy announced Simon's name as one of the substitutes.

A record audience from all over the world tuned-in their television as the two sides made their way onto the pitch. Tony had been true to his word and Sir Robert had reserved a seat for Nelson Mandela next to his own in the Royal Box. As Tony led his players out into a wall of sound he gave the President a wave. Mandela gave him a thumbs-up sign and waved back.

United had not dared to believe that Simon would not play and so Claudio Torrini lined up alongside Brad Finnighan in the centre of their midfield. At last the game was underway.

Liverpool's tactics were simple. They had decided to keep things tight and keep possession as much as possible. It was a hot sunny day and the plan was to make United run around as much as they could. They weren't too concerned about creating chances. That could come later. That could come when Simon came on, with half an hour to go.

In the first minute the ball flew out for a throw in and Tony jogged over to mark Finnighan.

"Lovely afternoon Brad."

"Get lost Hobbo."

Tony laughed. "By the way Brad, I'm fit today. We'll see shall we."

The opening exchanges were predictably tight and cagey. After ten minutes Liverpool's passing was humming nicely. They patiently moved the ball around the pitch and made the United players chase and harry. The crowd soon cottoned-on and every Liverpool pass was met with a loud cheer.

In the 21st minute a pass went astray. United grabbed possession and fizzed the ball forward. In a flash Finnighan was on the ball and sprinting for goal. Tony moved over to intercept. The Irishman dipped his shoulder and made to move left. Simon had quickly mastered this trick. The secret was to flick the ball right at the last minute. Tony had faced the trick over fifty times in the last fortnight. He calmly stayed on his feet and waited for the move. When it came he moved easily into the tackle and claimed the ball cleanly, whilst dumping Finnighan to the floor. He stopped and pushed a simple ball out to the full back. He turned and pulled the shocked-looking Irishman to his feet.

"Told you Brad. I'm fit today."

He read the Irishman a further three times in the first half and on each occasion he took the ball off him with ease. The confidence was beginning to drain out of Brad Finnighan.

Simon came out of the dugout twice during the first half and jogged up and down along the touchline. Both times the drums thumped into life.

"*Matembo! Matembo! MATEMBO!!*"

Tony sensed the nerves of the United players tighten a notch. They glanced over to Simon uneasily. Their self belief was slowly ebbing away. Liverpool were winning the mental battle.

The opening period of the second half brought more of the same. By the 60th minute United were starting to look tired. Their passes started to go astray and they were beginning to bicker with each other. Liverpool continued to calmly roll the ball around the pitch.

A sense of anticipation started to spread around the crowd. In the 68th minute Simon once again started to warm-up and this time the drums hit a new level of thunder. This time he would come on. Everyone knew it.

In the 70th minute the ball flew out for a Liverpool throw-in and Simon came on to deafening applause. The small tigerish figure of Claudio Torrini trotted over to stand close by. To everyone's surprise Simon took up a position between the two central defenders. For ten minutes he never moved out of defence. He jogged easily around pushing short passes to and from the defence and the midfield. Torrini followed him every step of the way and began to look slightly comical. On three occasions he attempted to sythe into Simon, but each time the African jumped out of the way with ease. In the 77th minute Tony gave him a small nod and he started trotting round in a circle behind the two centre halves. An embarrassed Torrini was forced to trot with him.

In the 79th minute Tony gave another small nod and Simon jogged back to his own corner flag and the Italian duly followed whilst Liverpool passed the ball around the midfield.

When he reached the corner flag he simply sat down. A tide of laughter poured down from the Liverpool fans who were massed behind the goal. For a moment Torrini simply stood and stared at him. He then shook his head in annoyance and ran back to the half-way line. In the 80th minute Tony gave another signal. This time it was open and loud. He threw his right arm up and yelled. "GO SIMON! NOW!"

Simon spun away from Torrini and sprinted down the right wing. The ball came to Tony who shaped to launch it towards him. The two United central-defenders charged over to block Simon's run. Finnighan launched himself into a desperate tackle to try and get the ball from Tony.

At the last second Tony dragged the ball back and Finnighan slid past. Tony then twisted his body and clipped his pass into the huge empty space that had opened on the left of the United defence.

Bobby Simms had timed his run to perfection. He collected the ball with ease and moved into the box without a defender in sight. He walloped the ball into the right hand corner and the ground erupted.

The Liverpool players mobbed Simms. They had practised the move for hours the week before and it had worked to perfection.

United were destroyed. They had fallen for a sucker-punch that had been coming for a whole fortnight. They made half-hearted efforts to get forward but they were a beaten side. Simon once again fell back to the defence. Liverpool caressed the ball around the pitch as their fans cheered every pass. United had given up chasing long before the ref at last blew his whistle for full-time.

The next twenty minutes were a blur for Tony. He lifted the trophy from Prince Charles. He shook hands with a beaming Nelson Mandela. He joined in the lap of honour as the team saluted their jubilant drum beating fans.

When he at last made it to the tunnel he was breathless with excitement. A hand grasped his shoulder. It was Andy Gray. "Not so fast Hobbo. You still owe me remember. Over here. I want an interview."

"No problems Andy." Tony shouted over to where Simon was celebrating with two of the younger players. "Hey! Simon! Over here!"

Simon came over and Tony draped his arm over his shoulder as the cameramen got ready. As he looked beyond the camera he saw a small group had gathered in the tunnel to watch them. Winston and his mother stood arm-in-arm with Karen and Ben. The Chief and Thomas were both beaming with delight. Next to them Samuel was holding Rose's hand and smiling a shy smile.

It had been a long road and a strange year but it had

ended in triumph. As Tony grinned at his family and friends his mind was filled with a single thought. "Could anything possibly ever be better than this."

A sharp voice pulled him back to reality.

It was a sharp Scottish voice. "Hobbo! Wake up will you! Right, we're on air - 3 - 2 - 1 . . . Tony, tell me, how long did it take you to develop those tactics . . . "

Outside the drums of Anfield beat on late into the London night.

The End